An Epic Life

Kev Richardson

A Wings ePress, Inc.

Historical Biolgraphy

Wings ePress, Inc.

Edited by: Karen Babcock
Copy Edited by: Jeanne Smith
Senior Editor: Patricia Evans
Executive Editor: Marilyn Kapp
Cover Artist: Kathy Williams

All rights reserved

Wings ePress Books
www.wingsepress.com

Copyright © 2010 by Kevin Richardson
ISBN-13: 978-1-59705-515-4
ISBN-10: 1-59705-515-8

Published In the United States Of America

Wings ePress Inc.
3000 N. Rock Road
Newton, KS 67114

What They Are Saying About

An Epic Life

5 Star Award!
A continuing **Kev Richardson** historical account of his extensive ancestral family tree, down through the evolving times of the industrial revolution brought on by steam-engines, hand-crafted train coaches and the ever-spreading spider-webbing of railroad tracks on the raw new continent of Australia. This author has an enchanting way of portraying the reality of living, breathing people behind the facts and dates found in your history books.

In *An Epic Life,* history shows in the mid 1800s, it became important to populate the British colonies' frontiers. It was a time in history when the number of sons was the only thing that ensured future prosperity. While adventurous men put their backs into the needed workforce to conquer the new land, the brave young brides did what they did best... kept house and bore new 'Littlies.' It was a harsh land, and not all of them survived, as the graveyards attest. It was a time when men and women braved the unknown to develop new territories.

Steam engines challenged the prospects of a meaningful future for those who recognized the importance of learning their letters and numbers. Education became more important than just for the elite. Even for those spunky enough to educate themselves, letter writing became one of the only ways to keep in touch with uprooted families, constantly on the move to wherever their work demanded they go.

After his father's untimely death, as the oldest child in the family, it fell to **Charles Allison Richardson** to face the responsibility of providing for his mother's family. Apprenticed at age twelve, Charles became fast chums with cousin Richard, and once educated in the service of the Royal Engineers, Charles set out to explore the new land, finding passage through the challenging terrain of the Blue Mountains. The family progresses to senior railway management.

Kev Richardson carries you through the laughter and pathos of a large family bent on taking care of its own. The integrated families have a proud history, and a bloodline to uphold. The story includes numerous nuptials, births and unexpected funerals. It was an era when loyal family members stuck together through thick and thin— happiness, contentment... or grief, determined to survive each new challenge.

JoEllen Conger
Conger Book Reviews, USA

Dedication

Soul, heart, and body, we thus singly name,
   Are not in love divisible and distinct,
   But each with each inseparably link'd.
                       Poet Laureate Alfred Austin's
                                Love's Trinity

* * *

Covers

Front cover photographs of Martha and Charles are from sepia prints found amongst the possessions of a descendant.

Back cover:

The print of the Lithgow Zig Zag, in its day the most ambitious switchback in the world, is from the original woodcut. It is reproduced courtesy *Australia's First Century*, Fine Art Press, Melbourne, 1988. Charles Richardson had significant input into its design and building.

The print of the significant *All-Saints, Brixworth*, Saxon built in the seventh century, is from a photograph by the author.

Disclaimer

Some names and characters depicted in this work are products of the author's imagination or are used fictitiously. Any resemblance to their personages' involvement in actual events, locales, organisations or persons, living or dead, is entirely coincidental and beyond the intent of the author.

Foreword

Dear Reader,

An Epic Life is a true tale of how lives reached across the globe, a major achievement in the mid-nineteenth century, where Charles and Martha carved for themselves a new dynasty.

It is not a rags-to-riches epic, although once drawn into the characters' minds, some equivalents are evident. Worldly influences on their transitory lives indeed enriched their minds. Together they unconsciously create magnetism, drawing people to them as they grasp at emerging opportunities to clamber out of a struggling existence. At least that is how their stories attracted me. I've tried putting myself in their shoes, reacting as they obviously did, for their lives to follow recorded facts.

All in the extended family were engrossed in the development of the railway, the discovery to revolutionise both time and travel throughout the British world. Other nations spent entire generations catching up on Britain's rocket-like surge into the emerging modern lifestyle, and this tale illustrates how particular people could be caught up in the whirlwind that whisked Great Britain into the most powerful nineteenth-century nation.

A historian writing about real people finds recorded in a motley array of government archives and family diaries, dates and places pointing the directions of his characters' lives. Yet when the events happened over a hundred years ago, we can but hypothesise on what occupied their minds—about what happened in their private worlds—about how and why they were drawn into the situations recorded as "events" in their lives.

All we in fact know about Charles and Martha are events—birth, marriage and death records, surviving census results, and regional archive reports. So to now write a credible tale honouring them and their achievements, the parts they played in creating true history, we must suffer the guilt of making assumptions on their personalities, loves, hates and goals.

Both were born into an England where life was either happily comfortable or boringly mundane, depending from which angle one chooses to look back on such times. By the early 1800s in Britain, with the industrial revolution so much in its infancy that it was yet unrecognised, a middle class was emerging. Cottage industry and subsistence farming under serfdom were giving way to industry. Having at last defeated Napoleon and progressed, with by then the world's strongest navy, the United Kingdom was fast becoming recognised as the world's strongest nation. The time was indeed an unprecedented period of change.

In the very year the story you are about to consume, the world's first steam-driven railway came into existence to accelerate changes in the world.

Charles and Martha were caught up in that maelstrom.

~ * ~

Fortunately I was not alone in compiling the data to tell their story. Valerie Greenhalgh of Brisbane and the late Desolie Lady Hurley of Sydney gave immense help in providing trinkets, photographs and diaries their great-grandparents left. I have simply tried sorting these crumbs into a readable tract, a posthumous acknowledgement of a job exceedingly well done.

Sincerely,
Kev Richardson

An Epic Life

BOOK 1

*Northamptonshire,
Yorkshire and Scotland*

Preface

England during the late 1820s and early '30s was a time of exciting change.

George Stephenson became a household name when his steam engine towed a wooden carriage on his newly designed iron tracks in County Durham, the twenty-five miles from Stockton-on-Tees to Darlington. There had been several years of horse-drawn carriages on rails—yet the steam train was one of the great marvels of the world. Nobody realised that it would kick-start all Europe's mechanical industries into a revolution. Steam became an entirely new concept of manufacture.

Yet whilst it was, in the long run, to provide considerable service to consumers as well as to a rush of mechanical invention that was ever to escalate, the industrial revolution was to take a terrible toll on all but the already wealthy. Factories began replacing cottage industries. Yesterday's nimble fingers at home fell idle as mass-production in factories increased. Craftsmen of tomorrow's world must acquire new skills—be engineers, mechanics, designers of machines which cast countless millions around the world, into gutters. There became two or three generations of people having to leave the land and move to cities in search of income, cities where noise and smoke began polluting both atmosphere and people's lives. Many sleepy villages of centuries found themselves transforming into smoky towns, and former pretty towns into ugly cities.

Today we realise the revolution still rages, electronics having replaced steam, that it is unstoppable, that we head willy-nilly to a lifestyle on which we can only postulate. We approach a situation similar to that which arose then. We realise that if the revolution is not checked, it must destroy so many of our pleasures—yet we do nowt but what our ancestors did—we tarry, persist in waiting to ward off life-threatening trends, until tomorrow.

In the 1820s, there could, however, be no waiting. The people then had no concept of the changes beginning to alter lives. Several generations suffered the pain of sudden poverty, children proving cheaper labour than fathers, working for pennies while their parents fell idle. Only painfully slowly could families find themselves able to begin climbing the rungs of recovery—the less educated taking the longest and suffering most. And education yet remained available for only those who could afford it.

During the eccentric King William's reign, following the death of his brother George IV, Lord Grey and his Whigs came to power. The King declared he would not interfere with Whig plans to introduce parliamentary reform, yet years of conflict followed with Whigs and Tories jostling for power. So reforms were few, the Slavery Abolition Act being the only major achievement while the increasing number of poor continued to be sacrificed as machines robbed them of use*ful*ness—left them to sit forlorn, pondering on the realisation that the rest of their life was to embrace use*less*ness. Their families would starve. The uneducated turned to stealing, petty crime leading, in turn, to the nation's prisons quickly overflowing. The government answer was to simply despatch further offenders, in chains, to the antipodes.

In London only, there was plenty of labouring work available as the nation was beginning to build train lines. It needed great, arched viaducts—navvies were laying a hundred thousand bricks a day...

"All very well for them up in London," the rural jobless cried, "but wot about us down 'ere?"

Only in rural areas where coal could be mined were labouring jobs available for the uneducated. And the uneducated, in a time before schools, was the majority.

One

Northampton City, 1839

Charles Richardson sat on his bed listening to the hall clock strike the half-hour.

That'll be half-five, I'd reckon.

His mind felt 'betwixt and between'—it had been a traumatic day for them all.

It's not just Pa's passing. We were ready for that. Six months we watched him suffer, get more tired each day, more abject at being able to do even less for us. What really recks me is that Ma seemed unable to wait more than five minutes after Uncle John and his family left for Brixworth to sit me down to tell me the next sorry bit of news. I know that as the eldest son, I am the one to give up lessons and go out to work—yet I guess I should consider myself lucky, as she says, that Uncle John can give me a job. Apprenticed at twelve? A lifetime as a carpenter? A cabinet-maker? A fixer of chairs?

He settled his gaze on the crippled chair beside his bed that his ma had sat on while giving him the news. His sisters had all sat on the foot of his bed, listening, twins Harriett and Julia, older than Charles, and Mary-Anne and Eliza, younger. Younger brother Fred had gone straight back to lessons after the funeral, while Uncle John and his tribe had come back to the house for an 'after-wake.'

Why didn't Uncle John take the chair back with him? I'd told him it was broke, that it needed a new leg. Ma made excuses for him, of course...

"He forgot, that's all, son. He and your pa were the closest any two brothers could be, and it was as traumatic for him as for us, to see your pa lowered into that grave. He even told me he felt some guilt in agreeing that it be your pa who was the best one to move to the city to find orders for the workshop."

Charles knew the story—that when a factory started up in Birmingham, making furniture by machine, the cost was less than if it were craftsmen made—that the Brixworth Richardsons had to restructure their business. His pa had been unmarried then, with no family to keep.

The workshop had, up until then, supported not only all Pa's brothers, but their older sons; and now it's reduced to only Uncle John and his two sons. And now me.

I can see Ma is upset that I must give up lessons—leave the learning to Fred while I make money. I know how difficult Pa found things, reduced to tending the Rectory garden for a few shillings, the workshop up in Brixworth making 'one-off' quality cabinets and chairs that Pa could find orders for. But then if he hadn't come to the city, Ma, me, and the rest of us wouldn't even be here.

"Am I to take over weeding the gardens at the church, then?" he had asked when his ma said he must go out to work.

"No, boy," she had said with a sigh. "Rector told me a queue formed as soon as Pa fell ill."

Diseased kidneys, the doctor told us it was. We all knew it would only be a matter of time. And he was not a really old man—fifty-something. Then she told me Uncle John would take me in—I'd move to Brixworth and live-in with his family.

"The Rector is to pay me a stipend for doing his family laundry and cleaning the church," she had said, "and with Harriett and Julia now earning, it's enough to feed us and keep Fred with the tutor."

Charles smiled to himself... *That's when baby John began struggling to get off her lap, and the chair took yet a further lean as she put him down on the floor.*

I'll not like leaving home, but I know it for the best. A twelve-year-old can't find work in the city, and Brixworth is but four miles off. And I like Uncle John. And cousin Richard is all but my age. He reads near as well as me, so I'll be in good company. And woodworking is all right.

Charles had always liked working with his hands, and he was aware of the alternatives...

Scrounging around with the rest of the city's twelve-year-olds for whatever work can be found—most of which is meaningless stuff. At least carpentry is a career.

He was old enough to begin realising he must start looking at things from practical angles—*else it would have been Fred having to give up classes, and then I'd feel guilty.*

~ * ~

Brington, Northants

The Billing name is today given to lanes, roads, and even Northampton City's major thoroughfare as well as to the nearby township of Great Billing.

In Martha's time, however, the Billings were humble, particularly in the then delightfully picturesque rural village of Brington. She grew up unwitting of the brewing changes brought about by the industrial revolution. She was given no reason to consider the centuries of history during which the Billing name graced the district. Her ma had persistently told how her ma, in turn, was a Burgess. "A worthy family, the Burgesses," she had ever insisted.

Certainly it's an elegant house grandfather Burgess lives in—with its many servants.

"It's in Brixworth, where I was born," Martha would tell friends as they romped or plucked wildflowers on the Brington common.

She often pondered on Brixworth, not solely because it was the seat of her mother's family, but on the fact that her pa seldom journeyed there with them... *Only when it's a funeral, it seems. And it's but four* miles along the road—not as if it were so far away it would take more than a day for us to visit—even with Mary and Thomas.

She wasn't to realise that her pa simply wasn't welcome there. It was only years later that she learned how her ma had been so captivated by the high-spirited Billy Billing from neighbouring Brington, then employed as roustabout on the Burgess farm, that she found herself pregnant to him. Squire Burgess had insisted they marry.

"No Burgess daughter ever bred a bastard child," he lectured her.

Then later, before his daughter's children grew to believe Brixworth might be 'Billing territory,' he prevailed on Billy Billing, whom he would never willingly recognise as a son-in-law, to leave Brixworth. "Take your family back to your own village," he declared.

Martha, but a toddling tot when the family was exiled, had grown up considering her pa's debonair mannerisms merely exuberance. She failed to recognise them as his expressions of his mind's fantasies. Yet she did sense that her ma ever seemed to live in a world uncomfortable, despite always illustrating a strong sense of love for them all. There was, however, in her pa's nature, something little Martha did recognise: his ever-eager attentiveness to her ma's comfort as well as to the family in general. All in all, it was a happy family.

And Ma always calls him William when everyone else seems happy enough, as does Pa himself, with Billy.

Yet Martha never wondered why—it was something she had simply grown up accepting as one of life's 'norms.' What she did wonder about, although realising it must be a serious matter or her ma would not insist on evading a clear answer when asked, was why her pa never journeyed with them to Brixworth.

Maybe to do with why Grandfather Burgess never even talks to Pa at funerals? It just seems so sad that he doesn't see the good sides of Pa's nature, especially when Pa is really the easiest person in the world to feel happy with—despite the sadness I know he and Ma feel at having lost so many children.

Questions on that was another area her parents seemed reticent to talk on. At eight and youngest in the family, a loving yet strugglingly frugal one, Martha had invariably felt lonely. Fifteen-year-old Thomas and thirteen-year-old Mary found her too young to be worthy of attention, so they sought the company of friends their own ages.

Yet she was an aware child. Aware enough to realise the different parental influences that guided her, her mother's landed background and her father's servile one.

With a little of both, however, Martha was to find, even if unwittingly, that it made her better able to cope with what her future had in store.

Mama seems ever coaxing not only me to adopt attitudes of greater awareness of 'being,' but Pa.

She had pondered on that point since first beginning to take conscious note of things her ma told her, things to prepare her for later life—such a one that even her wayward Pa could never even fantasize over.

Two

When Vikings were raiding English counties and salting the grist of their genes into Saxons, Brixworth's church of All Saints was already old.

It dominated the village skyline. It was not only the nation's largest surviving Saxon building, but the oldest still servicing mankind.

This architectural pearl of history, is what Martha's ma called it.

"It is not only where you were baptised, my child, but where I was baptised, and married, as your forebears have been for more generations than your mind can imagine."

On the first page of its surviving written records, dated 1568 during the reign of Good Queen Bess, is penned not only the burial of an Agnes Bray, Bray being the parental line of Martha's Burgess family, but that of the wedding in 1572 of a John Richardson, the family name Martha was destined to bear for all her adult life. So the significant All Saints would, for her entire life, represent a notable sense of belonging.

By the time she had grown up under the influences of both her father's Billing background and her mother's Burgess background to reach her sixteenth birthday, she had been well versed by her ma in both her Burgess and Bray roots.

"In fact, child," her mother would instruct on private occasions, private, that was, when out of Billy's hearing, "my Grandmother Burgess was herself born a Bray; so there is a proud history in your bloodline that you must endeavour to always uphold."

Ma's voice would always, then, adopt the condescending tone…

Martha had come to distinguish her ma's different tones over the years.

…and she would carry on with *"Yet you also benefit, my dear, from inheriting Billing blood. Your dear father has contributed a generous enough helping of quixotic dare-devilry to equip you for adventure."* Then she would look over a shoulder to be doubly sure *Pa couldn't hear, before adding, "I hope, however, that cautious Bray genes will provide you more balance in how you use your Billing genes, my girl, than your dear Papa tends to illustrate."*

Martha had ever wondered, after such counselling, over the meaning of all that. It ever sounded meaningful, yet its main innuendos left her still in quandary. And she was further hindered in finding answers by having no reading skills. Yet she had, at such times, become astute in assessing at least a sense of meaning from her ma's demeanour.

Mama doesn't seem to realise how difficult understanding some things can be. She was taught to read—"a Burgess indulgence," she calls it, yet cannot convince Pa that his daughters should be tutored. Only Thomas has been given some letters. "A girl needs only to know how to keep her husband's home—how to cook and sew," says Pa. "You learn those things from your mother, girl, and take heed of her bearing and womanly niceties so you can one day make a fine wife for a gentleman."

So how am I to progress? Mama tries, but then I know she has to do Pa's bidding, he who himself never learned to read or write.

Martha became conscious, as she grew, of her ma subtly coaxing her pa to strive for greater pride, consciousness in what she called the 'niceties of life.' Martha wondered if this were the role of every wife—

if that is what underlays Ma's references to the differences between Billings and Burgesses?

When at five or six, she reckoned it must have been, she discovered the sadness of death. It was when her brother Billy died at eight months. It had seemed so wrong, she could only sense, that such a tiny baby should be taken before having a chance to see something of life. Watching the tiny coffin being lowered into its hole in All Saints' graveyard alongside the tiny graves of brothers Joseph 1, Joseph 2, and Joseph 3 was one of the saddest things she'd ever witnessed.

The three Josephs had all been buried before she was born—*each, no doubt, in as tiny a coffin!* She would then wonder if all babies named Joseph died before having a chance to grow, and if it took all three of those deaths for her parents to realise it.

That they named their next son Thomas, and that he was still alive, had ever since stuck in Martha's mind.

She had overheard, at little Billy's burial, Grandpa Billing talking to Ma and Pa, an arm around Ma's shoulder, saying how sad it was that four of her seven children had now died before attaining even their first birthday. Martha had always, since, considered it fortunate that she had herself passed that dangerous benchmark—even wondered that, as it had happened to her Ma, might it also be destined for her?

Life can be very worrying… she had often pondered.

Then when Grandpa Burgess died at eighty-three, she felt it much more proper about life—*or rather death*—when graves were dug to grown-up size… *and certainly more proper when the one who's died has achieved so many years!* She felt less guilty, then, about being left alive while others died. She simply felt it strange how God didn't seem to take age into consideration when deciding who to take.

Bray and Burgess graves were, by then, spread throughout the Brixworth graveyard, but the only Billing graves were those of the three little Josephs and their brother William. It was shortly after that, she now recalled, that the family moved to Brington.

And, she further recalled when thinking back on that time, how it had seemed during her life, that there were far more frequent funerals for family at All Saints than baptisms or marriages. *Should I, then, when I marry, try to ensure I don't make Brixworth my home?*

~ * ~

Brixworth, several years later

Charles was pleased to be going home for Christmas. A year in Brixworth had been long enough for him to become as familiar with being parted from close kin as with learning to live with an adopting family.

He could now see why his Uncle John had been his father's closest brother in both age and companionship—they were so much the same in so many ways. His pa had one time explained the tradition of their line, how every generation called its first son after its grandfather and the next after its father, so Williams and Johns, throughout the district, dominated. Charles' father had been a William, so now Charles found his Uncle John surrogate father.

Why my own pa broke that tradition I've never known—yet always felt it too sensitive a question to ask.

Charles had been quickly followed by brother Frederick, and then it was a further nine long years before the third son, born only a year before William's own death, that the John name was conferred.

So am I now expected to name my first son, William?

Fourteen-year-old Charles consigned that problem to the 'too hard' basket. There was plenty of time before having to worry about that sort of thing. However, he felt highly satisfied at having been made so welcome in his uncle's home, where he had many cousins. William and John were oldest, yet it was third son Richard who was Charles' close friend and now, in the circumstance, a reasonable substitute for brother Fred.

So he felt pretty much at home in Brixworth. And enjoyed his work.

On Christmas Eve he journeyed to Northampton, tail-boarding on a neighbour's dray, to spend the family's modest festivities at Broad Lane. Yet there, gloom remained heavily evident.

"Oh, how you've grown in even these few months," his mother welcomed him after smothering him in kisses.

Ah, but, dear Ma, how you've aged... She was looking tired indeed.

"Harriett has been unwell for a time. She has the cough."

Julia, Harriett's twin, standing behind their ma, frowned and shook her head.

I'll find out the fullness of this later, then. He would not press his ma on it.

But then aloud, he said, "And you look well, Ma. And how about Mary-Anne and Eliza, and little John?"

"We are all well, boy. The girls have taken John to the common to get some sunshine. We'll be glad when winter is over. We had snow a week ago. Did you get that?"

He nodded. "But it wasn't much."

Their Christmas dinner was frugal. Eliza took time out from helping in the kitchen to take Charles aside—she told him how helpful the shillings he sent with itinerant tradesmen each week, were proving—and how worried both she and Harriett were getting about their ma's health.

"She does laundry at the Rectory three days a week for not only the family but for the entire choir. Other days she cleans the church, and is paid wretched little by way of coin. Harriett and I have found work in the new cotton mill, but now Harriett is kept to her bed, and Mary-Anne must tend her while me and Ma are at work."

"I've brought eggs and vegetables that should last you a week. And I've a guinea from Uncle John to put under the tree for Ma."

"Ah! She can pay the arrears on the rent with that. It worries her that they will ask us to leave. And we now have the doctor to pay for Harriett. But we know you can't give more than you give now."

She took a quick look over her shoulder. "Mary-Anne has knitted you a scarf. It will be under the tree tomorrow. So that will save you something."

"I'll be fourteen come July, Julia. Uncle John has promised me an increase. He seems pleased with what I do. I've already hived off the cleaning to the littlies, and I'm now scrubbing down timber. Uncle John says my learning has put me ahead of his boys in arithmetic, so I help him measure up. And I'm learning to trace patterns. We do mostly one-off pieces that factory production cannot cope with, so he gets good money from manors in surrounding villages. My future there looks good."

Then as Julia squeezed his hand, Harriett began coughing.

"She doesn't want you to see her until I've sponged her and done her hair. But she's excited about you coming."

Julia left to tend Harriett.

Yes, it's good being home again, despite the dour turn in their lives.

And Harriett, when he saw her, looked desperately ill.

"Influenza, the doctor says," she told him.

He glanced at his ma and Julia. All knew influenza was a serious complaint from which few recovered. Too often it turned to pneumonia, and once that happened, everyone knew, even prayers couldn't help. So after dinner they talked long and hard about the family future—until Charles held up his hand for attention…

"I was saving this for tomorrow as my present for you, Julia. But after what I see here, I will tell you now…"

He felt perky, being the bearer of good tidings.

"Uncle John has been asked if he knows a suitable maid for the big Burgess House. People are now calling it The Manor."

All the women threw hands to cheeks.

"Uncle John told them Julia should be interviewed. So, my dear sister, if you care to travel with me to Brixworth when I return, it being a Sunday, he will take you to the Burgess house. If suitable, you will live in, with keep, with every second Sunday off, and be paid two shillings for every day you work."

He sat back, looking smug while all looked goggled-eyed at each other. He knew they considered it a fortune.

Julia was the first to grab the reality of it. She clasped his hands.

"But surely, Charles, there are girls aplenty in Brixworth? Girls the Burgess family knows?"

"They don't want to be seen playing favourites. Cousin William's current hoyden is the dairy-maid there—"

"Charles," his mother exclaimed. "Such language! Is that what Uncle John is teaching you?"

Charles laughed. "No indeed, Mama. But that's what we boys bait William with. She is no hoyden. In fact, he complains she is winning the 'hard to get' game."

"Well good for her, son. Because if 'hoyden' is the sort of influence Julia would be exposed to if going there, then she does not go, two shillings a day or not!"

The conversation quickly straightened itself out as Charles explained how his aunt would keep a mothering eye on Julia.

"Brixworth, Ma, is not Northampton. Everybody knows everybody else, and morals need be kept in careful check or family feuds start. That's how it's been explained to me."

Yet all were cautioned by Mother Mary not to get too excited.

"If Julia can come home to say she has the position, that will be time enough for celebrations."

Three

How embarrassing having to admit my middle name to that census-taker!

Why couldn't Ma have had a boy's name rather than Allison? She insists that when she and Pa decided to dub me with it, it was compensation for her having to sacrifice it when she married. 'Charles Allison'—what a name for a man to wear all his life! I swore I would never admit it to anyone. Nor shall I! Census-takers, it seems, however, have God-given rights—he insisted on seeing my baptism certificate...

And now all my cousins rag me over it.

But then, I guess, it's but a farthing in the scheme of things. Burying our Harriett last year was as sad as burying Pa. And she knew she was going. Told us, she did.

"Get a message to Charles and Julia," she told Ma. "And please put me near Pa."

Julia and me went that very day, and she died that very night. The nice part of it was that she so loved that church. Of all of us, she was the 'churchy' one—had ever been chuffed at it being a circular church. She made a study of it, had the rector explain how it was called St. Sepulchre because it was a replica of the St. Sepulchre built by the Crusaders in the Holy Land. So we know she'll be happy there. And Ma and Pa were married there.

Charles often let his mind wander back on things while waiting for sleep—things both encouraging to think on and some ever to remain disappointments. He knew it wasn't in his own best interests to dwell on unpleasant things.

But it's hard to ignore them when they run counter to a fellow's nature.

He knew he had a hard streak, what some would call a mean one.

Yet doesn't everybody? And mine aren't really bad ones, maybe just a trite selfish. But how else is a fellow going to achieve if not a trite selfish? Why shouldn't a boy want to hive unpleasant things on to others if it's going to help him get ahead? It's those who stand back that see another jump in quick, to grab whatever advantage is up for the taking.

He had a quiet giggle. *Why shouldn't I use sharp elbows to get in first if it's going to help me get ahead?*

He had one time heard an orator use the 'sharp elbows' expression, and it had stuck in his mind. He thought it a 'cute' phrase and didn't mind borrowing it.

He shared a bedroom with cousins William, John, and Richard, invariably chatting about things to do with the workshop or on village gossip—on which village maid seemed heading for the 'hoyden' tag and which was trying to evade it. The latter was a subject that all four ever found something to giggle over. Even Julia, being a newcomer, was a target. Deference was paid to Charles in that respect, of course. And it had quickly become obvious that cousin William found Julia more than simply attractive. And that was good news to Charles...

...him keeping careful watch when other village blades are trying to make inroads takes some of the onus off me. And off Aunt and Uncle. And she certainly enjoys her work at the Manor.

~ * ~

Martha Billing had met Julia when Charles, delegated by Uncle John, brought her for interview.

Martha had herself arrived to work at the Manor when the crotchety 'Old Man' Burgess died. His eldest son, Martha's Uncle Robert, inherited. He immediately declared a restoration programme.

"For too long, the house and farm have been neglected," he announced.

And his sister Sarah's daughter over in Brington was called in for interview.

"At nineteen, Martha, you are old enough to understudy the housekeeper. She can't have too long to live, and I wish to retire her. So make the most of still having her around for the next month. And with my family moving in, you'll need to hire a further housemaid and a kitchen-maid."

So it had been Martha who approached John Richardson, who recommended Julia as housemaid. And Martha was taken with Julia. Much the same age, they established a ready rapport.

"I am glad you have some letters," Martha said. "With the old housekeeper gone, I need someone close who can read and write, for I cannot."

"I learned from my father and brothers," Julia replied.

"When I have children, Julia, I will see that all are given education. It is a changing world and becoming clear that it is people with education who get the best work in the new factories. My own father, without education, I saw being quickly passed over in favour of those more fortunate."

Neither related the modern outlook of the nation's young women to the fact that their entire kingdom had only so recently seen an eighteen-year-old queen ascend the throne. The young Queen Victoria had immediately begun introducing changes to tradition, many of them favourable to women. Had both Martha and Julia benefits of foresight, they would already know that the nation would discover a whole new world of feminism was beginning to develop.

"I shall not rule from St. James," the young queen declared to shocked advisers. "Buckingham Palace will become the Royal Residence." And it seemed no time before further announcing that she would marry so the nation would not again be left without heirs, should she suffer an early death. Then she made a further announcement to really shock the still stunned advisers: "And I shall choose my own husband."

She then, when their shock had somewhat subsided, declared she had already chosen.

"I shall marry Prince Albert of Saxe-Coburg-Gothe. He will be my Prince Consort."

And she quickly married him.

Martha and Julia looked on with admiration, each making private pacts with their own alter-egos.

Whatever opportunities emerge for greater independence than tradition has, to date, destined for women, I shall, of my own volition, eagerly grasp.

Four

For Edward John Bourn, the national capital was proving a far different world from Kent, despite its Canterbury being hardly rural. His family was one of industry and learning rather than pastoral, yet young Ed, even with such a background, found adapting to the world's biggest city a mammoth challenge.

He was highly educated and had followed his father into the burgeoning railway-coach industry. The advent of the steam engine near twenty years ago had seen the railway industry mushroom overnight. Lines were being laid throughout Britain and its colonies at frantic speed, so coach-building skills were in ever-increasing demand. His father, an engineer by profession, had recognised the potential for not only mechanical skills in the new industry in which he had found himself a career niche, but growing peripheral areas—including coach-building in the Bourn hometown of Canterbury.

He apprenticed his only son into that side of the wider industry, and young Ed, having qualified in both coach design and construction, had been successful in applying for a position with Britain's largest railway-coach builder, Wright Brothers of London and Birmingham.

As the industrial revolution mushroomed, he joined the great migration of young men migrating from rural towns and villages to major manufacturing centres. At age twenty, he farewelled his parents and seven sisters and took a train to London. His parents had been loathe to see their first-born and only son leave home, yet they were of the new breed of family that recognised the need for sons to be led by career opportunities in their changing world.

His mother had hailed from London's Shoreditch where her 'aunt,' dear friend of her own parents over years, had offered to provide lodgings for Ed. Shoreditch was a comfortable distance of Wright Brothers' Battersea plant, so young Ed Bourn and the widow Rawes' daughter, Maggie, became quickly attracted.

Maggie Rawes was also of 'good' family. Her father had been one of Savile Row's most eminent tailors. Maggie, baptised at the fashionable St. Clement Danes on London's Strand, just around the corner from her home, had also received advanced education. They found each other suited in many respects, so it was not long before marriage plans were in the air.

"We should take the Herbert Street house, Maggie. It seems the best of those offering. It is commodious enough to take in your mother and still have room for numerous children."

Maggie, surprised by her Ed's so forward an utterance, looked to see if Mother Rawes were listening—and only when realising it safe, emitted a quiet giggle.

She and Ed had spent much of Sunday inspecting houses, and both considered 98 Herbert Street in Shoreditch adequate.

Maggie's papa had been deceased some years, yet his ghost still lingered in most rooms of the Rawes' Shoreditch house where Maggie had, for most of those years, with all siblings having married and gone, cared for her mother. It had been Ed's suggestion that Mother Rawes now let the house go and move in with the newly-weds.

"Let's face it, Maggie," Ed had ventured, "your ma is sixty-something, and having weathered your father's foibles for near forty years as first live-in companion to his first wife, she now illustrates frailty."

Maggie agreed. "She should not find such a move a wrench, it being but a block from where she's lived since dear Papa retired. She will remain close to friends and even closer to Papa when she wants to take fresh flowers for his grave."

Gerard Rawes was buried at St. John the Baptist. Maggie, however, preferred the more social St. Leonards for her own marriage. And so it was. After a week's honeymoon in a Brighton Hotel, her Mother Rawes moved into their Wenlock Street house.

~ * ~

Charles and Julia rode the post-stage to Northampton.

Their mother was marrying again.

Fred had written Charles to affirm what the brothers had assessed on Charles' previous visit, that their Ma seemed to be positively responding to the attentions being paid by widower James Tear, the local cobbler. He had a workshop and retail outlet near the church.

"They are to be married at St. Sepulchre, Charles," Fred explained. "And of course she wants you and Julia to be here."

It was three years since their father died, and with both Charles and Julia able to send regular sums to Mother Mary, she had been able to keep Fred in studies and provide a healthy and happy home for the three younger ones. Work hours in Brixworth had proved long, and whilst neither Charles nor Julia had met their soon-to-be-stepfather, Fred and Mary-Anne insisted that marriage would take much pressure off Ma.

So on their arrival at Broad Lane, a festive air prevailed.

"Romance seems to be in the air for more than one in our family, Ma," Julia announced as they sipped tea after lunch.

Even young John looked up, surprised.

Charles gave his elder sister a wry smile.

"And who then, is he or, she?" asked Ma.

"My brother Charles here is courting a Burgess maiden."

Charles simply sat waiting. He wasn't surprised at Julia's announcement.

"A Burgess maid?" asked young John.

"No, silly. I am the Burgess maid. Your brother is courting the housekeeper. She is Burgess born."

"She is Billing born," Charles corrected.

He then explained to the others that it was Martha's mother who was Burgess born.

"But courting is hardly apt," he continued. "We have done no more than walk home from church together the last few Sundays."

"Well, Martha talks with me about it," Julia added. "She asks ceaseless questions about our Charles. She leaves me with little doubt she feels you are courting her."

"We talk about local things," Charles explained as if defensively. "She knows all Brixworth's Richardson families, particularly Uncle John's."

"She's several years older than Charles—what if..."

"She is three years older, but insists that both her mother and grandmother married younger men..." Then he hastened to add, "Not that the thought of marriage has been raised. She has simply explained that women of her family, when it comes to friendships, seem to prefer the company of younger rather than older men."

Mother Mary smiled. "Well that certainly didn't apply in this family. Your father was twelve years my senior."

"And your second husband, Ma? Is he older or younger? And has he children?"

"He is older, and both his children are married. They live in Long Buckby, James' home before moving to the city. Long Buckby is known as a shoe-making village."

Charles knew it. It was but an hour's drive away.

"But tell us about your Martha," Fred insisted. "And how appropriate is Julia's 'courting' expression? You, brother, are but seventeen—hardly old enough to be thinking of marriage and supporting a family."

"True indeed, Fred. But I am not courting. I enjoy her company, yet only as a friend. She is simply easy to be with, not as awkward as I'd thought the company of women would be. Her father is from Billing, although she is Brixworth born—her father worked on the Burgess estate; they moved back to Billing when she was still small. She was asked back to Brixworth when the Burgess housekeeper retired."

"We share a room," Julia told them, "and talk about the young men of the village. That's how I know she thinks fondly of my dear brother."

"Well, she has a long wait if she has marriage in mind. I'm not ready for such responsibility. The cost of a wife is, alone, enough to deter me. I don't even have a career yet. And who knows—Richard and I are even talking about joining the Royal Engineers so we can travel. And we can't do that until eighteen."

Everyone looked surprised.

"Why the Engineers?" Fred asked.

"It's where you get paid for learning a trade. And travel goes with it. They teach you on location—wherever the trade takes you. And they pay to dress and feed you. We haven't decided yet, but we're agreed it's something worth thinking on."

"Have you talked with Uncle John on it?"

"No, Ma. And we won't, yet. But we know the furniture business can't support too many of us. Richard has two older brothers, and I'm an outsider. So it makes sense that he and I look elsewhere for our futures."

~ * ~

Martha Billing was in a flap.

Oh what can I do? Charles comes into my life, and for the first time I'm victim of discovering what a young man can do for a girl's dreams. Ah—let me rephrase that—a woman's dreams. Yes, at twenty, I am a woman. Yet men my age are of no interest. Here is a young man with promise—promise in the way he sees things— promise in that nowhere in either Brington or Brixworth have I known anyone who seems to have plans towards a future—let alone a future illustrating a reasoning mind, a mind like Mama's. If it were a mind like Father's, he wouldn't interest me at all. Dear Pa hasn't the mettle to grasp opportunity. Charles, whether he realises it or not, shows that he has. I see how dear Mama has ever wished her man were worth looking up to in a gentlemanly sense. Lately, however, I realise how she has relegated that hope to wanting only to make him, and her children, happy. She seems to have lost her will to influence her own marriage. In dear Papa I can see what attracted her to him—his dare-devil approach to everything, his intuitive rashness—or should that be 'brashness'?—his so natural wont of inspirational urges no matter how lacking in any real common sense.

But Charles Richardson? He illustrates promise, the promise of someone I could feel more at home with than with even dear Papa. With Papa there is ever a sense of question; with Charles the sense is purpose and direction—enough to enthuse me. I feel his life is something I want to be part of, not in a mothering sense but in a supportive sense, to be part of it with him.

And that the Richardson history in Brixworth rivals both the Bray and Burgess families is a further feather in my shaft's vane. Oh dear God, please let me convey to him my eagerness to be part of his life, before he discovers some other girl. Or woman.

Five

The Corps of Royal Engineers was a proud contingent founded in 1717.

However, once into combat, it was realised that lack of qualified hands to design and erect ramparts, bridges, and other engineering aids in winning engagements, as battle techniques changed, was a setback. A unit of Royal Sappers and Miners was added.

Once turned eighteen, Charles and Richard Richardson joined the Corps, encouraged by their respective families, who recognised the advantages of such a move for ambitious young men in troubled economic times. With the country no longer at war, the Corps embraced not only the science of military ordnance but the plotting of railway routes for the burgeoning locomotion industry. Charles' Uncle John agreed it was a good move for the boys.

"The RE has a proud history, Martha," Charles told her. "It fought in the Crimean War, and a detachment of Royal Military Artificers as they then called the Sappers, went to train the Turks against Napoleon."

"Will you be sent to a war, then, if you join?"

"It's highly likely. However, right now, no war threatens. Furthest we'll be sent will be Wales or Scotland, I should think..."

Little did either realise what an enormous understatement was such a prophecy to prove.

"...But that is still travel, still seeing new territories. And there'll be work aplenty for years to come. We even receive extra pay if working away from home."

So the two new Royal Engineers left home and families for the Royal School of Military Engineering at Chatham in far-off Kent. And passing through London, never having been in such a large city, they felt for so long after entering its outskirts that it was never going to end. The exuberance of discovering such adventure betrayed the insular lives both had lived during all their eighteen years.

It was the exuberance of young men still raw lads at heart.

And the challenges of army life, disciplined study, and demanding schedules, kept them 'heads down and tails up' for an entire year—with no time off for travelling back to explore London, let alone for visiting family. Yet their comradeship strengthened, and both made firm friends of others of their age—friends with similar goals.

They learned much about people. Each had grown up with everybody around them familiar. Now meeting strangers, they found that, too, an exciting new challenge.

Charles couldn't help but feel the tinge of selfishness lurking inside him was taking on more of a rosy hue.

What's amiss then, in a fellow feeling smug about how his life is turning out?

He found it interesting how, whilst entertaining considerable empathy in respect of a number of his new friends, he was still conscious of a sense of 'self' in respect of them—even wondered that if a time should come in his future when it came to a situation of 'them or me', would he be prepared to avoid trying to create some advantage, that he could use it against them?

Would that be cheating? Or simply winning at one-upmanship!

He put it on the shelf. There was no call to be making such a decision now.

Yet his new friends were creating a new awareness in him.

"There be more strange people in the world, Ric, than I ever suspected. Arthur, for instance, hailing from Cornwall—have you ever heard such a weird accent? I can hardly believe it's English that he's talking…"

"And Walter. 'Geordie' he calls the way he speaks…"

"Tom calls his 'Scouse'. You and me, Ric, are the only two in our entire class who speaks proper English. What sort of schools can they have in those places, I wonder?"

Charles and Richard were beginning to realise that Northamptonshire wasn't at all the centre of the world—everywhere else but a series of tangents.

~ * ~

Martha and Julia giggled quietly as they lay in their cots, the space between them in their attic room no more than three or four feet, little enough that if in whispers, staff in the next room were not disturbed; the two could comfortably exchange confidences and gossip.

Julia's workday was usually over by the time the Manor's family finished dinner. During it she would tidy up their private rooms for whenever they wished to retire. She would then repair to the kitchen for her own supper and to chat with the rest of the staff.

Martha's day, normal for a housekeeper, ended only once the rest of the staff was fed and retired. Only then could she ensure the house was properly secured and generally ready for the family to come down for breakfast. Julia had begun helping her with those final chores so they could retire together. Then while preparing for sleep, they would discuss the day's events, and increasingly often, personal feelings on their own morés.

Martha in particular found the developing friendship of benefit. She had never had a sister close enough in age or interests to fulfil such a role. She envied Julia the fortune of having for all her early life a sister so close as to be a twin.

Not that I wish on myself the prospect of bearing twins so two daughters can be close—surely birth will be painful enough without carrying, let alone bearing, two at once. And raising two at once. Yet I hope my daughters can be closer in age as they grow than Mary and me.

She had never failed to rue that difference. Now, at last, she had found Julia.

Or is it that she is now lonely, having lost that sister? Am I nowt but someone to fill that need for her?

Whether it was or not, Martha's desire to be fulfilling the need was such that she refused to bother over the reason. So the friendship developed into an ever-strengthening bond, one she would remain protective of. And the subject they were right now giggling over was Martha's interest in Julia's brother.

"Not only is Charles tall and handsome, Julia, but he carries himself with a pride I do not see in other men. Or maybe 'pride' is not the right word; there are two meanings to it, of course. Mine is the nice one. He illustrates a self-confidence that is not misplaced—and it is a deserved confidence. He seems to know where he is going in life, an outlook I've never noticed in Brington or Brixworth men."

"But he is indeed a Brixworth man, Martha. Our father was as much a Brixworth family as your mama's. Had he not moved to the city in his youth, Martha, you and I could even have become sisters."

Such a thought created more giggling. Yet Julia was indeed happy to find Martha confessing an interest in her brother. She was impressed by Martha and also entirely happy that their friendship continued developing. In fact Julia had already pledged in her mind to do all possible in furthering both those interests.

"Of course he is yet only eighteen, Martha. If you are thinking of romance, let alone marriage, I'm sure you will find his heart is yet dedicated to the army. His last letter to me said he will be home for Christmas, after which the Corps will despatch him to field-work somewhere. So other than at Christmas, which he will want to spend with Ma in the city, you cannot be seeing much of him for quite a time."

"Oh, that disappoints me. You will simply have to engineer, Julia, that he spends as much time here in Brixworth, come Christmas, as he can. Please, Julia? Please?"

~ * ~

On Christmas Eve, Charles stayed in Northampton on arriving from the academy, while cousin Richard proceeded on to Brixworth.

At Broad Lane he was met by a toddling little stepsister. His ma had given stepfather James a daughter who, on yet unsteady feet, grasped Charles' knee as he played with her. Little Alice was indeed intrigued with the colours and stripes of his uniform.

Brother John, now an exuberant eight-year-old, had several inches added to his height. Charles was hugged by not only his mother but sisters Mary-Ann and Eliza, and brother Fred. James Tear greeted him cordially, with the firmest of handshakes.

And he was pleased at his mother looking considerably improved in health.

And Mary was as impressed with how her son had grown.

"You look so handsome, boy," she insisted. "The uniform is indeed smart."

He always felt jaunty in it, so wore it proudly.

"You must wear it when we go to Brixworth for New Year," Julia insisted. "I have arranged that we travel there to have New Year with Uncle John and his family. I have to return to work by then anyway. I will ensure you wear that cap at just the right angle."

She took care to make no mention of Martha and certainly kept secret the connivance by which it had been arranged.

"The world is indeed changing, Ma," Charles told his mother. "London is a bustling metropolis..." He paused to let that new word he had learned, have its effect. And indeed, all seemed bemused by it.

"Horse-drawn trams are large coaches moving people about the city. The city is so large that distances are too great to travel by foot. These trams ply the major streets, while trains of three and four carriages carry people down to country centres—drawn by huge locomotives blowing whistles to alert people and traffic at crossings. Each one leaves behind it billowing clouds of smoke from the fires under the boilers that power them. And they even created a tunnel beneath the river Thames—an underwater road. Isn't that amazing?"

Mother Mary felt so proud for him...

So grown up, he has so quickly become. If his father were still here he would indeed be proud; there is so much more adult in him than in any other nineteen-year-old around these parts.

The entire family attended church on Christmas Day and spent the next two days in animated conversation and good feasting. Charles and Julia then took the stage to Brixworth.

Charles would spend several more days with his 'adopting' family before he and Richard returned to Chatham. Julia was returning to immediate work at the Burgess house. She had personally laundered Charles' 'star-spangled' uniform, now carefully packed in his valise, to wear when calling at the Manor.

An invitation for him to visit—"To see where your sister works," had already been 'orchestrated.'

"Be sure to come to the servants' entry, Charles. I want to check your uniform before you meet the family. I'm sure they will all be impressed."

Charles also looked forward to the meeting. He recalled his meetings with Martha, since which time he had given her considerable thought. Richard had since told him something of the gossip surrounding the Billy Billing presence in the town and how, when Martha was but a child, her father had been despatched to Brington.

He recalled having discussed with Martha the coincidence of both having moved to Brixworth to take up residence and employment with respective uncles.

"In my case, Charles," she had said, "it's been a returning to where I was born. In your case it is to where your father was born."

She's obviously been delving into my family background then... he now also recalled. He gave little instinctive attention, however, to the fact that village life ever seemed naturally built around its families' histories.

His reunion with his Brixworth family proved as welcoming as arrival at Broad Lane, yet on the first occasion that he was able to draw cousin Richard aside, he whispered, "Julia has arranged for me to visit the Manor, Ric. I am eager to see Martha again."

During their year together they had confided on Charles' interest in Martha. "She's a girl to simply feel at-home with," Charles had insisted.

"Girl?" Ric had countered with. "She's hardly a girl any more, Charles. She must be twenty-something! I still cannot understand any man having a feel for an older woman."

"She would have turned twenty-three only in October, Ric."

"Well you're only nineteen. If you were to marry her, she would age more quickly than you."

"I shall be twenty come July. And my Ma's just told me how much I've aged during this past year. She made a point of telling me that. And if Martha and I find enjoyment in each other's company, who is to say we are not better suited than those of like age? She told me her mother was five years older than her father—and they remain happy. Her parents are welcome again at the Manor now that her Burgess grandfather is dead, so you may well get an opportunity to judge that for yourself."

"You seem well versed on her family. Is a real romance in the air, then? Are you thinking of proposing to her?"

Charles smiled.

I'm not going to answer that. Firstly, until I've seen Martha again to assess if she is still keen, I don't even know if interest will continue. And if it does, I might still just keep Ric guessing. In fact, I want to first see what is going to happen to Ric and me now we've graduated. If we are sent off somewhere distant on field-work I will have to be separated from anyone of interest, so pursuing such a course is something I can't rush into. And I certainly yet cannot afford to even think of keeping a wife. I've simply to keep an open mind on all that.

But he certainly had in mind the possibility of a future with Martha.

Or is it only because Ric has prematurely jumped to such a conclusion? Is it that, that's got my mind in such a whirl?

Six

In 1847, Britain insisted it was not at war. However, it was understandable that families with sons being sacrificed in repelling armies trying to save homelands from being colonised by the now greatest military power on earth could not be convinced.

Newspapers were daily proclaiming 'successes' against the Sikhs in India's Punjab and against the Bantu in southern Africa.

"Sweeping victory," the *London Times* assured readers as more and more lands were wrested from reigning Moguls on the Asian sub-continent. Also considered a victory, according to the press, was the consolation prize of at last agreeing with the Americans on a division of which lands should be British and which American. A line was simply drawn along the map at the forty-ninth parallel. North of it was affirmed the British colony of Canada, whilst south Britain had to lick its wounds from having lost the American War of Independence. It could do nowt more now than stand back and watch the United States assert its own territorial advances against Mexico. Latest annexation on that front had been the territory of New Mexico.

It was indeed a time of powerful nations simply seeing the riches of the rest of the world like a flower garden that could be raided at will—ripe for harvesting, plucking this bloom or that on a first-come-first-served basis. Every large, worldly nation was proving as guilty as the others.

Whilst the industrial revolution had inflicted considerable hardship on the poor at home, collecting the fruits of colonial expansion to feed the machinery brought each stronger nation increasing wealth. The RE had units just behind the various front lines in Britain's several bloody conflicts yet, fortunately for Charles and his mates, not the units surveying railroads.

On return to work after the several days granted them over Christmas and New Year, Charles and Richard were told their unit was being despatched to the west-midlands.

Shropshire's rustic town of Crewe already had a branch line operating from Birmingham, and it had been established that Crewe was to be Britain's major rail junction.

"Looks just like a spider getting ready to pounce, Ric," remarked Charles when a map of the proposed lines emanating from Crewe was pinned up on the wall of their classroom. From the black blob marked 'Crewe,' six lines projecting from it did indeed look like the outline of a large spider. Due north, the line to the port of Liverpool was already in service, as was the line south to Swansea, Bristol, and other south coast ports. East was the present line through Derby to the North Sea, and southeast was to Birmingham and London. The line west as far as Chester had been laid five years, and the RE was to now survey from there the near two hundred miles along the north coast of Wales, to Holyhead.

"We shall travel to Chester by train, lads," they were told, to respond with rousing cheers, "although don't expect to be travelling first class. That is for generals."

The lads didn't mind. Hard wooden seats and glassless windows weren't insufferable hardships when taking into consideration that the journey would take only a quarter of the time by a coach-and-four.

"But you will need to take care, lads. Soot and ashes will be blowing into your eyes without stop."

First-class coaches had roofs, so were positioned at the rear. Science had established that soot and ashes from high smoke-stacks blew more safely over the carriages immediately following the engine, so carriages without roofs occupied that position.

"Single men will bivouac first at Chester, then move on to Colwyn Bay as we work westward. Quarters for married couples are established at Bangor, and those men will work eastward"— Lieutenant Smyth removed his monocle to stare at all and sundry—"and if the lines working west and those working east don't meet up with perfect precision, someone's going to find his balls being used for cricket!"

There were ripples of laughter. Charles looked across at his friend Arthur. Arthur and his Annie had organised their wedding during the Christmas week, for all had been told that provision was made for married men on field-work. Arthur sat with a satisfied smirk on his face—a sort of—"So I won't be the target of snide remarks from you mates if I show up late for work any morning."

Charles had grinned.

I now know I'm going to marry Martha Billing. I know she is keen on me—Julia told me that even if I couldn't see it for myself. But I'm not marrying at nineteen. I've said nowt to Martha on it one way or another because I want to leave options on timing open. However, after my week with Julia, I reckon she and Martha have each other's ear on things like this. So I don't have to raise things with Martha in future—I can simply hint things into my sister's ears.

So he would be careful, in future, to put just enough in his letters to Julia to ensure the furnace remained fuelled enough that it wouldn't die. And in his letters to Martha, which he now realised it would be more likely Julia reading them to her than anyone else, he would not now have the difficulty of worrying how overt or obscure he need keep what he considered 'encouragements.'

But I'll talk with Arthur along the way. We'll be on this assignment the best part of a year, they say, so with no time off for travelling home, there will be opportunities aplenty for me to sort my mind around romance.

~ * ~

Martha missed Charles.

"Since seeing him at Christmas, Julia, I am more sure than ever that I want him. Has he said anything to you?"

They were turning in for the night.

"No, but don't be disappointed. You've seen the glow in his eyes when he's with you. He's being careful not to say anything to me one way or the other. He knows we talk. He just wants time yet. And more savings behind him. He'll be writing to me, for I made him promise. I'll keep asking subtle questions."

"It's times like this I really suffer being unable to write. But then— if I could, I'm sure I wouldn't know how to put things in case he gets the wrong impression. But I miss him. Will you tell him that for me?"

"Of course, if that's what you want."

Julia could almost sense Martha's anguish. She felt it strange. She was only a year younger than Martha, yet had never yet had the yearning over boys that most of her friends had. She wanted a family, yet had ever been of the mind there was plenty of time ahead.

Of course that could change if I find the man I want. Like Martha.

But Martha didn't see herself so different from Julia.

Julia's man hasn't walked into her life yet. But mine has. He's younger than me, yet old for his age. Mama's always said girls are mentally older than boys. "Some say that never changes as time passes," *she would add, yet I wonder if she thinks that in her situation—Pa never really caught up to her? Even I can see that. I don't see Charles as younger than me because we seem on equal footings. He gives an air of being versed in the ways of the world, yet I know he's not seen any more of it than me. I'm always conscious of feeling ill-versed. I've been cloistered as much as any Catholic nun, hobbled by Pa's un-worldly ways. Mama isn't like that, so is that aura something gained from having education?*

She stared at Julia, not smiling, rather illustrating determination.

"Can you teach me write?"

"One first must learn to read. Only once you have even a little skill there, the science of writing is easier. Reading helps you understand how to use the language—gives you a feel for composition. Trying to write when you don't know how to compose thoughts would be difficult. Fred has his reading manual—I shall ask him next time I'm home if I can borrow it. But your father? You told me he has strong feelings about a woman learning to read and write."

Martha put on her determined expression. "He doesn't have to know!"

Julia smiled again. "That's the side of you I wish you'd show more often."

Martha knew there was a determined streak in her, somewhere.

~ * ~

January was bitterly cold, and whilst he found the salt air invigorating, Charles didn't enjoy working by the seashore. Howling winds blowing sleet into his face were twice as strong as anything at home.

"So bitter it would turn sugar sour," he told Ric

And fingers manipulating intricate machinery had to be bare; woollen gloves weren't conducive to setting sensitive instruments.

"How can a man take readings when visibility is but a yard?" he asked Lieutenant Smyth. "It was never as cold as this when we learned it in the classroom."

Lt. Smyth couldn't smile. He wore the thickest moustache Charles thought he had ever seen, and right now it was frozen. Charles could only think how painful it must be.

The weather was so untoward that work was called off.

"Back to Chester, lads. If things improve overnight, we'll make an early start tomorrow."

Bloody hell! Should a man feel that the penalty of getting home out of this tempest means an earlier start in the morning?

He looked at Ric as they seated themselves in the wagon, but one of Ric's eyes seemed frozen shut.

"I was on the spectroscope," Ric shouted. He had to shout to be heard over the roar of the wind. "My eyelid stuck to it."

So they had problems in the field.

What an intro-bloody-duction! A man's first sight of bloody ocean in his life, and what does he get? No wonder the navy is troubled with tars deserting.

"Our schedule calls for four miles a week, lads," they were told back at base. "And the Brass in Chatham ain't concerned about weather. They got pot-boilers in every office to keep their-selves warm and their tea on the boil. What we didn't get finished today we must make up. If we get behind, you're goin' ter find yerselves workin' twelve hours a day through summer when you could otherwise be playin' football on the beach. So you got to make every mile count."

"Bloody all-right for them, mates, they can wear mittens while they write their reports. We're the ones out in the weather."

"Jesus, mates,"—this from Walter in his Geordie accent—"even the bloody convicts in Botany Bay don't have this sort of weather to work in. Do yer reckon they'll start floggin' us if we fall behind?"

Some laughed.

"I wonder if they're looking for surveyors in Botany Bay, where it's forever warm? Now there's a thought," Charles posed.

"Let's break into the mess to nick some blankets," Ric responded. "Do you think we might be lucky enough to get transported?"

Surveying wasn't proving all 'beer and skittles.'

By April, however, the weather was less averse to work comforts, and morale was somewhat restored, as was their schedule. After church muster on Sundays, the progress against the work target was reported, and teamwork was proving its worth. Already it was obvious that, saving some unforeseen calamity, they would meet their target come year end. They worked seven-hour days, six days a week, and by August, reports showed, with the progress the western group was making and the progress the eastern group was making, they should meet ahead of schedule. None could imagine that the following winter could deliver worse conditions than last. So morale continued to improve. The eastern unit had already transferred to their new bivouac at Colwyn Bay.

However, in early September, Charles was sent for.

"Maybe you're for Botany Bay," Ric joked.

When he arrived at the office, he found his mates Walter and Tom, and another good fellow, Henry, had also been summoned.

"We are transferring you," they were told. "There's an urgent line to be laid in Yorkshire. We are ahead of schedule here, so you lads are to go there. You four have been chosen from this group, and Arthur Vincent will be joining you from the western group. You will join lads from other groups there."

"Richard not on the list?"

"No. Your cousin is not."

Charles showed his disappointment. "We've been together since joining the Corps, sir. We're family. Can this be reviewed?"

His captain's response was a stare over the top of his glasses.

"I've been given these four names, and these are the four who will go. If Richard wants to submit a transfer request, he can do so, but it would have to be a life-or-death situation to bring about change. Maybe at the end of this assignment, he can request a transfer."

Charles could only suffer disappointment. He'd never thought he and Richard might be separated. And another problem was in his mind... In his cot that night his head spun.

How long is the Yorkshire tenure? I had in mind that maybe at the end of this stretch, a year from now, I could look at Martha and me marrying. By then I'll be twenty-one. But could this Yorkshire job be another eighteen months or two years?

Certainly with his increased pay-rate once taking to the field, and with his keep found, he would be in a better financial position to keep Martha...

But does the 'wife' accommodation come free? I'll ask Arthur about that. He'll have his Annie with him. So if Martha and I marry before going to Yorkshire, she will have Annie's company.

He resolved to get to the captain as early tomorrow as possible, to ask the timing of the transfer. He was now eager to find out exactly when he would be meeting up with Arthur.

Seven

At breakfast next morning, mail was delivered—a letter from Julia, short yet on two significant matters.

Their ma was unwell—she was expecting another baby and having a difficult time. *The doctor has ordered her to bed for the duration of her time*, it read. *She is allowed on her feet for an hour or two each day, for exercise and a little sun when the weather is kind.*

Bloody hell, he thought... *Ma pregnant again? We were all amazed when she told us she was expecting Alice—not usual for a woman of forty-three. We were sure Alice would be her last. But now? At forty-five?*

The second news was that Martha was missing him... *She hopes you can by now have some news as to when you might be home for a visit—she sends her love...*

Ah! Love? Oh, what a wonderful word! But is it Martha's choice or Julia's?

He wanted it to be Martha's. He felt all a-tingle.

"Wow!" he said to Ric. "Here was I even wondering if, because of our long separation, her interest might be waning. Now she sends love!"

He was now doubly anxious to get to the captain.

"Sure I need to see Ma. But who knows, mate? I might even marry Martha..."

His voice trailed off—the now immediate likelihood of such a momentous event, struck him as a reality...

Up to now it's been but something only 'possible.' Suddenly it's something that can happen within weeks! Oh dear God, what sort of date will the captain expect me back in Yorkshire?

The door to a life with Martha was no longer ajar—*It's wide-bloody-open! As real as that today is Thursday. Within a handful of days I could be sitting with her, planning a wedding? Oh, and she'll want to marry in Brixworth—in her All Saints, the dream of any Saxon girl. For Martha, of course, it's not only where she was baptised but where her parents married—and her mother's family baptised, married, and buried over centuries...*

But the news of his ma's illness was the heavy weight on his mind.

Ma will want to be at my wedding. How can I bring myself to ask her to risk her own well-being by journeying to Brixworth? And if well enough to travel only the two blocks from Broad Lane to St. Sepulchre, it means Martha must forego marrying in her family church. Mmmm!

There were moments of dilemma in his mind when thinking of Martha having to leave home, family and heritage for the wilds of Yorkshire...

He sat back. *I shall simply inform her that is the way it must be.*

Yet his mind all too quickly returned to his own situation on their future. *And after that... What? Anywhere for the rest of our lives at the whim of the RE?*

Through his mind flashed the fact that all his children would have no traditional birthplace, no traditional home to be married in—buried in when their times came... *My career could have us ever on the move.*

And doubts on any one thing quickly became overshadowed by bigger doubts as further factors sprang to mind. *...But what is Ric on about? My mind is in such a whirl I simply haven't been listening.*

"...so that is something else you will have to be keeping mind," Ric was saying.

Charles sighed. "Sorry, Ric. My mind was adrift. What were you saying?"

Ric raised his eyes to the ceiling.

"I was saying you need to keep in mind that you mightn't always have me by you to bounce things around with. Seems they're going to keep me here in Wales while you go to Yorkshire. What is it, seven years we've been together, sharing the growing pains? I shall miss you."

"And I you, dear friend—I've ever felt fortunate in that parted from my brother, you were here to fill the gap. We've both benefited. I too will find parting a wrench."

"Maybe you'll have Martha to fill your gap?"

"Who knows? I've yet to find out what my immediate future is. I must find out the Northampton situation with Ma on the one hand and Martha on the other."

So he was still in trepidation as he waited in the captain's anteroom—to five minutes later be told his transfer to Yorkshire was effective immediately.

"Various small private railways have been operating East Yorkshire for some time," he was told, "some still horse-drawn and overall, several different rail gauges. Even canal boats are moving coal from various mines, and fabrics from cotton mills, to various river ports. The entire system is being nationalised. The government will build standard gauge all the way from Leeds to Hull—and connecting lines north and south from Selby. Your new bivouac will be Goole."

All that sounded fine to Charles, subject to the timing of his transfer. He had no idea where was Goole other than that it must be somewhere near Leeds.

"But the timing, sir." He held out his letter. "I have news only this morning that my mother is ill. And I had been planning to marry..."

He didn't mind stretching truth if it were to make it easier to sort out his problems.

"I would dearly appreciate a spot of leave if it could be arranged during the transfer."

"How long do you want?"

"Two weeks?"

"One. Go see your mother and attend to family duties there. When is your marriage planned?"

"I don't know, sir, but I could find out the answer during this visit."

"Where is home?"

"Northampton, sir."

"Two days there and two days to Goole leaves three days for your business. I'll have the staff sergeant give you a pass from Saturday. It will entitle you to second-class travel on all lines."

He dismissed Charles with a wave of the hand.

He believed himself lucky. *Many an engineer has not been so fortunate in requesting compassionate leave.*

"Because it still fits in with the captain's leeway on the transfer," Ric told him on the trolley speeding them to their field site. "But are you thinking of marrying within those three days? To straight-way leave for Goole? And I cannot be at your wedding?"

"No, Ric. I am not thinking of marrying so quickly. All I can do is get to Brixworth and propose. If she says 'Yes,' then we must wait until I know my work schedule."

On arrival he scribbled a note to Julia and Martha, telling them he would be at Broad Lane Tuesday and Brixworth Wednesday—that he must depart Northampton early Thursday for Leeds. He wrote also to brother Fred at Broad Lane, with his love to Ma. "I can have an overnight with you," he wrote.

He posted the letters at Conwy when they broke for lunch.

"Maybe I can spend a night with your family, Ric. It all depends if the early coach from Brixworth on Thursday can get me to Northampton in time for the train north. I can check that on arrival at Northampton. Or there again, maybe I can arrange to tail-board from Brixworth to get me to the train on time."

Next day he called to the staff sergeant's office for his pass. He there checked the ordnance map for Goole—it was on the junction of the Don River from Doncaster and the Ouse.

That night, Richard helped him pack.

~ * ~

It was suppertime Tuesday evening when he arrived at Broad Lane.

His two-day journey on the road... *or on the rail, is more to the point,* he told his embattled mind, had been exasperating. He had left Colwyn Bay at dawn, rugged up to ride the trolley all the way to Chester. Whilst thankful he didn't have to contribute to manning the crank, he couldn't help but feel sorry for the navvies who did. They knew he needed to catch the noon train for Crewe. Even from there, he had fingers crossed that he could still make Northampton by tomorrow afternoon.

How much of it I can do on my rail pass is in the lap of the gods— and I have no more confidence in them as even in these two guys puffing and panting trying to get me to the first leg.

Nor did he know how frequently trains left Crewe on the Stoke-on-Trent line. Nobody at the bivouac had known the timetable from there to Northampton.

"It's on the main Crewe-to-London line," was all one of the lads could tell him.

If the worst comes to the worst, I can take a stage. But that would put me hours behind the train—that's assuming, of course, there isn't a breakdown.

And he had little faith in the hope of there being none. Railway breakdowns were more common around the countryside than expecting one could arrive according to schedules.

'Timetable of Lost Causes' had become the sniggered nickname given the Railway Timetable that kept getting recalled for amending and reprinting.

'Emending' they should be calling it, he reckoned. He had looked it up once, the difference between *amend* and *emend*... *Correct, make better, as against seek to remove errors—how does a man qualify such a subtle difference? Or should that be 'quantify'?*

Either way, he was left unsure.

Yet when it refers to endeavours to keep Britain's growing railway timetable up to date, it should more likely be emend. 'Seeking to' seems more apt to what our railway planners are about.

RE men, of course, their responsibilities complete even before rails were laid, could afford to be cynical when it came to pointing fingers at causes of railway mishaps.

Yet where faults lay was not his current concern. He couldn't afford having 'failed to report for duty' appended to his service record come next week. His week's leave had been made out to end on a Saturday. So he had a day up his sleeve in that Sundays were rest-days by RE law. He didn't have to front up to work until Monday morning.

Yet RE workdays begin at eight, by which time a man has to be finished breakfast and assembled. So it's Sunday I must be in Goole. And do trains run on Sundays?

He made a mental note to check that out, although railway gossip had already satisfied his mind that yet on many lines whether a Wednesday train ever got to leave anywhere on a Wednesday depended largely on if it had arrived on Tuesday. So whether or not the London-to-Leeds line scheduled a train to even arrive Leeds on a Saturday or Sunday, having come through Northampton en-route, he still couldn't know.

All I can depend on now is that this trolley can make Chester before I miss the connection to Crewe.

He must take a hotel room overnight, if not at Crewe, then in Stoke-on-Trent.

And he made his connection, quite without the half-expected trauma.

His adrenaline settled considerably, and he was able to find a seat with his back to the engine, highly desirable when windows had no glass. Even with a roof, soot and sparks could easily blow into one's face. At Birmingham, the train waited long enough for passengers to drink a cup of tea and purchase a ready-made sandwich. During the break, he struck up a conversation with a travelling salesman, one at the 'aspiring to become a gentleman' stage of such a career. He sold books, popular novels of the day. He had been waiting to join the train, travelling only as far as Coventry.

"Gad," he declared when Charles told him he was in the RE, "what's the RE to do with surveying rail-routes? Aren't there enough wars to keep you busy, old chap?"

Charles chose not to humour him by offering a sensible answer. "We're cutting our teeth on railroads while waiting for war. If your train runs into a dead-end one day, you'll likely find it's because the country's been invaded and the RE's been seconded to defence, old coq!"

He felt chuffed from there on, so much so that he didn't mind at all when it began raining as they climbed a hill just out of Rugby. He didn't dare let his mind travel to the poor third-class passengers in carriages without even a roof, especially as the rain became really set in such that they lost an hour getting to Northampton because the wheels kept slipping.

He took a hansom to Broad Lane.

Eight

Mother Mary looked more drawn than he recalled her even when his pa died.

"You've got that bonnie bloom of an expectant mother in your cheeks, Ma," he lied. "So what's ailing you, eh?"

"You don't have to try bolstering me, boy. I know how I look. But how did you get time off to come and see me?"

He felt almost a flash of fear in her eyes.

Bloody hell—can she think she's so far gone they've given me compassionate leave?

"No, Ma. I am being transferred to Yorkshire. I get a few days off in between."

"What, Wales to here, then here to Yorkshire? None of us have ever been so far. All that in itself must be taking more than just a few days?"

"Trains are part of the world now, Ma—many times faster than horses. And they don't break down as often as coaches. And they carry twenty times the number of people. Tomorrow I go to Brixworth. I've messages of love from Richard to his family, and I want to see Julia and Martha."

"Martha's your young lady. Julia told me about her. Says she wouldn't be surprised if marriage is in the air. Is that why you're home?"

"It's you I've come to see. Julia told me you are abed. But yes, I want to see Martha too. Maybe marriage is in the air. We will talk about it tomorrow. But tell me about yourself. How far along the track are you?"

Mary giggled. "Along the track? I'm not a train, boy."

Then she raised a hand. "You're only trying to distract me, and I haven't finished about you and Martha. How do you know she is the right girl for you? I haven't met her."

Now Charles giggled. "Are you telling me, Ma, that I shouldn't be thinking of marrying any girl you haven't approved of?"

She reached out for his hand to squeeze.

"Maybe something like that. You can't understand what we call 'women's intuition.' It's a never-fail diagnosis."

"Never-fail, Ma? What if when you meet her, you don't like the one who loves me—isn't one of you failing? But that could not happen. Richard tells me Uncle John thinks we'll make a good match. And he grew up in the same village as Martha's ma—known her all her life— even knew Martha as a littlie. You will see it too, when you meet her."

"But you getting married, son... oh dear. My eldest boy. I do want to be there. Will you marry at St. Sepulchre? I could make it there."

He pulled a chair up to the bed and now put her other hand in his.

"She will want to marry at Brixworth. I will simply tell her that cannot be. We will marry at St. Sepulchre. When do you reckon my new brother is due?"

"It mightn't be a boy—you know that. After Christmas sometime. Most likely early January. But when a woman my age has a baby, it can come very early or very late. One never knows. I get a feel the doctor thinks I might lose it anyway."

"Has he said so?"

"Not to me. And if he's told it to James or your sisters, they're not saying. But I guess you'll follow that up. When do you go to Brixworth?"

"Tomorrow."

"And you'll come back here?"

"I hope so, for a quick visit Friday morning. It depends how early I can leave Brixworth. My train leaves at mid-day, so maybe I can squeeze in a half hour here."

She smiled. "Please try, son. I don't want to have to wait until Julia can visit to get your news."

Mary-Anne came in, then, with a tray bearing medicine.

"Outside with you now, Charles. Ma has to take her medicine and then sleep. She's already had early supper. Are you staying the night?"

"Is there a bed for me?"

"You can share with Fred. He's just come in if you want to talk with him."

"I sure do."

He kissed his ma's cheek.

"You have a quiet night, Ma. I'll serve your breakfast if nurse here will let me."

Mary-Anne poked out her tongue and giggled. Charles left her to tend their ma.

~ * ~

Martha was agog. She was not keyed up, but clued up. Friendship with Julia had developed into one of fully fledged confidence—she had come to realise how Julia had filled the gap surrounding her life.

Julia had proved as good as her word in searching out from other acquaintances printed historical tracts as subjects for learning to read. It became a pastime giving them many hours of togetherness once retired to their room. Martha was particularly interested in the published advice for young ladies wishing to learn the niceties of societal behaviour and habits.

"You never know, Julia—one of these days I might be invited to tea at the palace," she joked.

Their sisterhood relationship included the sharing of even personal confidences.

Queen Victoria had been on the throne long enough by now for the expression 'Victorian prudery' to be commonly used in social circles. Young women were realising it was important to be seen rather than overtly expressive about romantic desires, as bashful about them. Their minds should trend not on the 'overt' but on 'obscure' tendencies.

Yet sisterly confidences were considered private enough for taboos to be tolerated…

"…Even desirable," Martha and Julia were agreed.

"You will find, Martha dear,' whispered Julia when taking a 'time-out' in their studies on the eve of Charles' visit, "that my dear brother will have something particular in mind on this visit. It will likely be more than simply a social call. Cousin Richard wrote me that Charles has romance in mind."

Martha had clapped hands to her cheeks.

"Did he say more than just that? Oh I fear I shall now die of curiosity before he arrives."

Julia sat with lips pursed.

"Martha, dear, I wouldn't be at all surprised if, in the near future, you and I might truly be sisters."

"Oh don't by a tease, Julia. Tell me all that Richard wrote. Do you still have the letter? I didn't even know Richard was writing to you."

"I received it only yesterday. He said he hesitated over telling me, but he certainly seems to think Charles is hoping to hear something encouraging from you in respect of a future together. So there now— what do you make of that?"

Martha's hands moved from her cheeks as she crossed her arms over her breasts to hug her own shoulders. Julia could almost sense her friend's trembles.

"Tell me again what he said about his reasons for coming home. I had thought he was not getting leave until Christmas."

Julia fetched her letter from Charles.

I have a week's leave pending transfer to Yorkshire. I expect to be home Tuesday and will take the early stage to Brixworth Wednesday. I look forward to seeing you, dear sister. And there is a serious matter I am keen to discuss with Martha. I hope you can convince her to find time that we can talk in private. I may likely have to leave again same day. I also hope to find time to pay respects to Uncle John. I have messages for him from Richard.

"And that is my brother's entire letter, Martha."

So Martha, come morning, paid particular attention to her coiffure and had every intention of pinching colour into her cheeks as soon as she knew he had arrived. She had made Julia promise to let her know as soon as he came. She knew the stage arrived around ten or ten-thirty, and it should take Charles no more than ten minutes to walk to the Manor.

And having organised her work schedule so she could have an hour with Charles, she was already at the upstairs window with the best vantage of the direction the stage would come. She could not see it actually arrive, but from the guest-room window there was a gap between trees to the hilltop by All Saints where the road took a curve. Passengers would alight from the coach within ten minutes of that.

On seeing the coach, she ran to her Uncle Robert's library from where she would see Charles come through the gate. She waited impatiently.

He should have come by now—her heart gave little jumps—could something dreadful have happened and he missed the coach?

She knew Julia's ma was ill...

Could something utterly dreadful have happened there to keep my love from me?

But heart-flutters stopped as, several minutes later, Charles arrived.

Oh what a confident stride he has—such a determined gait he invariably has... Ah—he's carrying flowers. Yes, he dallied long enough to stop by the High Street florist.

She was so excited she forgot about pinching colour into her cheeks.

And did he choose to wear his uniform especially for me?

She felt so proud for him. And for herself.

Their greeting was reserved, for by arrangement, Julia was in the vestibule, as were the butler and another maid who Julia had warned to expect her brother.

It was a warm September, and there were no fires in the grates. And Martha, aware the family was attending the market fair, had ensured the staff would leave the parlour unattended and would lead Charles there.

But things didn't work quite like that.

Instead, she rushed to the vestibule to nearly melt at the smile on his face when he saw her. He bowed his head and gave her the flowers.

Without really seeing them, she gave them to the maid to put in water.

"Then please put them in my room," Martha asked. "Then bring tea for three to the parlour."

They chatted on Mother Mary during tea, Charles telling how he was due in Yorkshire by the weekend.

"It's never sure, of course, how long I will be on any one assignment, but the project in Yorkshire is scheduled for at least a year. Lines from all industrial centres in that part of the country are to connect en-route to Hull. And westward all the way to Leeds and Bradford. There's even to be a line all the way to Glasgow, so there seems several years of work for the Corps that I can look forward to."

"Oh, the excitement of all that travel, Charles—seeing all those new places."

"I'm not sure I'm looking forward to moving further north, Martha. Not with winter coming on."

They chatted on such mundane things until Julia took her leave.

"I'll leave you two together," she told them. "It seems you've much to talk about."

Charles patted the empty spot on the sofa beside him.

"Come sit here. I've something to tell you."

She shivered—*a nice shiver, though.* She sat beside him and put a hand on his. He took it in a firm clasp and held on is if to keep her from moving away...

...Oh! As if I would!

"I've no guarantee of getting Christmas leave," he began. "Last Christmas was after having completed my studies and graduated. Now in the field, we've been told that come mid-winter we will have further studies, so that could be through Christmas. And that far north means that in the event of thick snow, we could not travel anyway. And I want to... Well, what I am trying to say is...”

“What I want to say, Charles,” she hurriedly announced, as if needing to say it while he was so full of stumbles, “is that I would like to spend that winter with you—this winter and every winter...” She paused but little, squeezing his hand hard. “Is that what you had in mind?”

He appeared both flabbergasted and relieved. And inside, his heart pounded. *Julia has done her work well.* He was highly elated.

“Are you reading my mind, Martha? Because if you are, girl, you are right on track—full speed ahead, you are. That’s exactly what I was trying to find the words for. I practised, but they’ve gone clear out of my mind. I do indeed want to spend the rest of my life with you.”

He turned towards her now, taking her other hand and holding both in a hard enough grip that might have been painful...

...Which would be painful, her senses reminded her, *if my heart weren’t beating so fast I can’t feel anything else in the moment...*

He leaned forward quickly and kissed her on the nose. He wanted to clasp her entire body as tightly as he was clasping her hands—to kiss her deeply on the mouth—yet Victorian morals stayed him. He wondered how far he could go without shocking her, making her retract from what her words had promised.

She wanted the same, but couldn’t read his thoughts.

He told me before, that I can read his thoughts. Yet I cannot read them now. I want him to hug me tight, kiss me deeply, press hard against my breasts so I can feel his heartbeats? Oh, yes! Oh how sure I am that this is the man I want to spend my life with, he who is to be my lover, discover in my body the intimacies I am already aware of...

They spent a long time not talking, simply holding hands and searching each other’s face with their eyes. And when they did start talking again it was to illustrate that they had so much to say to each other, yet realised that until beginning to talk realities of the immediate future, they were, within an hour or two, to part again...

...for how long? We must talk about that now. We must make plans as to what we must do, what things we must put off until the future, how long must be the lonely interim...

Both, if only they could realise it, were now having exactly the same thought.

"Please marry me, Martha? Marry me quickly? The Corps has bivouac houses for married men—little houses to be sure, two or three rooms, while single men live in barracks. I am to leave tomorrow. Maybe if I can go back to ask for a week's leave to get married, I can then take you to Yorkshire? Arthur, one of my mates, is married. He and his Annie live in the married quarter, so you will have her for company while Arthur and I are away in the field. Or in school. I'm not sure how much is the 'wife allowance,' but I can find out next week. Yet with keep and rent found, it is obviously enough that others make do on it. I can't be rich for a time yet, girl, but who knows about the future? With all this unemployment about, at least in the army, I'm getting paid..."

His voice trailed off as if he'd suddenly realised how he was trying to answer all unknowns about the future in one burst...

"I don't know any of those things either, my dear one. Yet nor do I care. I'm not from a rich family. Even now, my father is unemployed. All army men's wives must manage, for there must be thousands of them. That's not going to be my worry. In fact I'm not going to have any worries about our future. Dear Charles, so long as I have you I will find ways around what you call 'wife problems.' I can push problems from me. I left a loving and caring family to come here to take a self-supporting job, just as if I were a man. And I've done well. I am a survivor, Charles. I can calculate risks, face problems. I've proved that to myself. And I can show you how I can be happy with whatever we must face together."

Charles couldn't believe he could be so lucky.

She's right, of course, that it's practical to have a sensible outlook, one many women have, I'd reckon, but few who have the experience to realise it. Or the mettle to handle it.

They talked, then, about marriage.

He worried about how he would overcome the problem of his ma not being well enough to travel to Brixworth. He had wracked his brain with worry, knowing that this would have to be faced.

"Martha, my dearest, there is a problem about having an early wedding. All Saints up there," and he pointed to it through the windows.

Martha put a finger to his lips. "I too have been thinking on that. Julia tells me how ill your ma is, and I know—"

He now interrupted her. "Julia has told you about Ma, then? That—"

She touched his lips again. "Please kiss me, Charles?"

Still seated, they clasped tightly and kissed, beginning gently, yet neither seeming willing to end it, pressing harder and harder, mouthing the most intimate kiss either had ever experienced and neither seeming willing to finish.

Yet at last they did, slowly.

She again put her finger to his lips.

"Julia and I have never discussed you and I marrying. Yes, she told me she suspected you might have romance in mind, but it never went further than that. She has told me your ma is exceedingly ill, carrying this baby. Is your question to do with your ma wanting to see you married?"

He was flabbergasted. *This girl really can read my mind!*

He nodded.

"I've dreamed of you asking me to marry you"—and she now moved her face forward to kiss him on the nose—"and yes, I want to marry you, and I would be far happier marrying you at your church, right by your ma's house, than marrying you in my own church, knowing she couldn't be here."

He hugged her again.

Whew! What a let-out is that!

"How can a man be so lucky as to be marrying a girl like you?"

She smiled.

"All Saints is where I was baptised. Julia tells me that St. Sepulchre is where you were baptised, so I don't see much difference. My family is all hale, all can travel from here and from Brington to the city. The only question remaining, my darling, is the 'when' of it. Have you some plan?"

"Can we think about October? If I go to Goole and ask my new captain for a week to get married, it might be best before I get too far along the track with a new outfit."

"I have a birthday in October."

"When?"

"Twenty-second."

"Would you like to marry on that day?"

She nodded.

"Then I'll ask for that time. I should get my answer straight away, so can write to you so you can make arrangements."

"Don't write to me, silly. Write to Julia."

"I'm going to teach you to write, girl. That's a promise."

She smiled. She had decided not to tell him that Julia was teaching her to read. She wanted to keep all that as a surprise once they were alone together as man and wife.

They kissed lovingly again before going to the kitchen, where Martha knew Julia would be waiting for their news.

Nine

"No!"

That was the first word Charles heard from his new C.O.

He had requested leave to be married in Northampton on 22 October.

Charles made a quick summation of his new captain.

Cold, raw, over-full of self-bloody-importance, wanting only to illustrate his power.

He realised it would be useless pleading.

This is a mechanical soldier, taught the hard lesson that a precedent is set if an officer concedes to a plea.

"When may I marry, sir?"

"Have you already got her pregnant?"

"No, sir."

"How can you be sure?"

"We have never fucked, sir."

The robot then actually smiled—all too briefly, however.

"Well you have mettle. Northampton, eh? You can train that in a day. So if you leave on a Friday, marry Saturday and return Sunday, you can have leave." He wrote out a pass. It read: *Depart on a Friday of his choosing, return Sunday.*

"Give this to your second corporal. Now get back to duty."

Second Corporal Martin Ohlsen was human. Charles liked the stamp of the fellow.

He read through the captain's note, then smiled.

"How far away from what you wanted, is this?"

"Several days sir. On what dates in October do Saturdays fall?"

"You've been lucky," he told Charles. "This is bloody reasonable by his standards. What date do you want?"

They walked to the wall where a calendar hung.

"Twenty-second, sir."

"Forget the 'sir' when there's no colour present."

He ran his finger down the Saturdays in October.

"Twenty-fourth. But that is a Rally date. How about the seventeenth?"

Every man must attend rallies.

The few days' difference is surely not going to worry Martha.

"Seventeenth."

"I'll give you a pass for departure Friday sixteenth through Sunday eighteenth."

He wrote out the pass and held it out. Charles took it, thanked him, then turned to leave.

"Oh, one more thing," Martin Ohlsen said.

Charles turned to find Ohlsen with his hand extended.

"Congratulations," he said.

~ * ~

Goole was a transit town and far from picturesque. He had imagined all river towns to be rural like the Constable he had seen on the only occasion he visited a gallery. But rather than fields and flowers in sunshine, it was a mixture of shipyards, warehouses, smoking steam-engines, and fish-markets against a backdrop threatening rain.

"The married-quarters bivouac is in the village of Whitgift, a couple of miles of town."

Yet Charles was having a difficult time trying to explain to the sergeant why he needed to know about married-quarter bivouacs when there was no wife.

"There is no wife yet," Charles explained, "but there will be in October. I want to book a house now so I'm sure of having one."

"A bloody Casanova, eh? Needing a bloody tryst to bring bar girls? That's the screwiest reason I've been given yet. Gettin' bloody married in October? I'm not goin' to fall for that one. Piss off."

Charles giggled inside—*sure it must look that way to him.*

"Well, you can't blame a bloke for trying." Then he showed him his leave-pass.

"Christ!" the fellow said. "You're the bloody type, that if there's another war, they'll give you general pips in the Secret Bloody Service. But good luck to you, mate—here..."

He filled Charles' information on a record, making sure the carbon paper was fresh enough to make the copy readable, assigning 'Bungalow 16' to it. He handed Charles the key.

"But if I hear it's being used for clandestine purposes, you'll cop it. And my lockup ain't too bloody comfortable."

~ * ~

St. Sepulchre, 17 Oct 1847

Charles Allison Richardson, having enjoyed his twentieth birthday only three months past, waited at the altar, tingling. His brother Fred stood by him. He had been trying for all the intervening months to grow a moustache, yet remained frustratingly disappointed. He wanted to look older. Or at least not too young for those who would critically look on his Martha as a young woman prepared to marry a man still so youthful.

Martha, five days prior to her twenty-fourth birthday, strode ever so confidently and proudly on Billy Billing's arm to where, under the soaring dome ceiling, Charles, Fred, and Ric waited. Billy stepped back so Julia and Martha's sister Mary could move to Martha's side.

Mother Mary, propped up on cushions in a front pew, her Jamie Tear beside her, her various children alongside tending little Alice, and Martha's mother and her Burgess family just across the aisle from them all, watched proudly and happily as the ceremony progressed.

The bride and groom of course, could remember less of the detail after it than could the guests; they were too intrigued with firstly the closeness of each other and, secondly, the intricacy of procedures. After the punch-line and the kissing of the bride, when the wedding party retired to the vestry for signing the register, Charles made his flourishing signature and Martha made her cross.

This cross has always stood for Martha Billing, she couldn't help but feel, *yet from here on this same sign is to represent Martha Richardson.*

She couldn't help but now realise how purposeless was a mark in representing who she really was. She couldn't wait to progress her skills to the stage of signing her name...

My new name!

~ * ~

They had married during a global whirlwind.

The mid-nineteenth century was a period of massive strides in the evolution of what was to be called the middle class. Great Britain was leading industrial change. The days of designating the populace as the rich on one hand and poor on the other became days of realising that the poor were beginning to divide into the very poor and the not-so-poor yet still not rich. These emerging families found they could buy at least a little of what their parents had ever considered luxuries for only the 'privileged.' What they failed to realise was that they were emerging from the heartbreak of unemployment in traditional life regimens, to discover usefulness in new.

The division of classes, it was quickly evident to those with a latent studious bent, fell largely into the category of those with some education and those with none. The new world of machinery called for new skills, and those who proved most adept at learning them were those already disciplined, even if but a little, in letters, numbers, reasoning, and planning. Some began picking up pens and working on further areas of people's lives where machinery could benefit, whilst others realised that, with serfdom being slowly strangled, there was room for middlemen in properly structuring the changes. The newly educated were reading what was happening beyond their eyesight, giving them encouragement in a new-fangled idea called self-help.

So there was considerable jostling between those who found room to manoeuvre when having to cope with change. Charles seemed able to change the pace of his strides into the new world without even realising it, and Martha, undoubtedly encouraged by having taken on the responsibilities of housekeeping for a gentle family at such an early age, was now eager to grasp each new experience being presented.

"Travel, Charles, is something I've never done. Brixworth to Brington and back again is my only experience; yet now I must not only travel to Yorkshire, but make my home there. It is like realising a dream on the one hand yet facing unknown challenges on the other. Yet I sense no fear, only, with you at my side, the magnet of adventure."

"There is no need for fear, girl, when we will be facing everything together. And at least under the British Army umbrella, I am saved the risk of venturing into areas of risk."

And for me, she thought, *no longer being alone will make strangeness easier to cope with. When Charles is in the field, sometimes for several days, he having said, I will be physically alone, yet aware that he will soon return. That will add expectation to life—expectation of something pleasantly familiar. So one simply cannot become lonely.*

The world now encouraged people to think more positively than those of earlier times.

After the ceremony and a night of anxious yet eager lovemaking, sometimes fervent yet still for many moments cautious, for it was new ground both trespassed on, Charles had to breakfast early before catching a train to get him to Leeds by nightfall. That gave him Sunday to reach Goole, not that the distance was great, merely some forty-five miles as the crow flies, yet he had no way of knowing even if trains ran on that branch-line on Sundays. If there were no coach he would hire a hack and ride. Such occasion would provide abundant time to replay the memories of his wedding day—not only the ceremony, but the mingling of families meeting for the first time, not to mention the euphoric exchanges during the night.

On that score he now felt happily secure. The traumas of fear attached to it now seemed to have been greater than warranted.

It was the not knowing, the fear that if our lovemaking had been disappointing, oh what a terrible dilemma of a future we then would have had to face.

He faced his new day positively, however, despite the disappointment of having to part again. *But at least with the knowledge that everything has gone so swimmingly, creating a confidence for our future.*

And Martha was as relieved and happy, for she had harboured the same dilemmas.

After breakfast at the inn by Northampton's rail station, she said, "I shall remember yesterday and last night for the rest of my life, my darling. All of yesterday will live in my mind as the happiest day of my life."

And their parting had to be brief.

"I should know within days, my dear, when you can come to join me. I will write you at the Manor. Julia will read it to you, and she has already promised to help you pack. Ma says you can spend the night at Broad Lane so Father James or Fred can see you on to the train. If I cannot meet you in Leeds, I'll organise someone to be there. Arthur's Annie will already have arrived, so it might be her. Whoever, they'll have you paged once the train has moved on."

Julia had already been appointed housekeeper at the Manor, so that left Martha without pangs of conscience at having to quickly surrender her responsibilities there.

And having already said my farewells to my Brington family, I can leave on whatever date Charles wants.

Meanwhile, as Charles' train pulled into Leeds station, he smiled.

Martha is absolutely agog at the thought of travelling by train, yet she is trying to pass it off as if not a particularly exciting adventure.

Ten

Six months after their marriage, Martha received a letter from home.

"Your grandfather Billing has died, dear," her mother wrote. "Ninety-one he reached, and still able to walk with a stick. Your pa is distraught for he loved him dearly. We are burying him here in Brington, and I entered your name on our wreath. The funeral will be Thursday, by which time you should have this letter. You may like to offer a prayer for his soul. He was a kindly man, though crotchety these latter years."

"Good strong stock, eh, my dear?" Charles quipped when finished reading it to her. "Maybe you might live so long so we can be Darby and Joan like those old folks."

"Well, if I do live to that age, Charles, I'll be crotchety too—which wouldn't be pleasant for you. But I doubt I will live so long. Nobody else in my families has lived to that sort of age. But yes, tomorrow I will offer him a prayer. He was ever kindly to me. When leaving Brington three years ago, on saying goodbye to him I thought it likely I'd not see him again."

That letter had been dated a week after Julia had written to say Mother Mary had had her baby.

"After all the sickness carrying it," she wrote, "it proved a comfortable birth, but it has left her weak. It is a boy they named James after his father."

"Forty-six she is, Martha. Have you ever known a woman to have a babe at forty-six?"

Martha shook her head. Charles did a quick mental calculation. "That makes it twenty-three years after bearing her first—a long time for any woman to be bearing."

Martha shivered.

"And her first were twins. I guess it's just as well we never know what lies in store. I just hope, my darling, I'm not still bearing when forty-six."

She held back the fact that her own parents buried their first three before any reached its first year. And then a later one.

And nor do I want that for Charles and me.

The next two years proved a happy time. On many occasions, they reminded each other how happy they found life. Every month, however, Martha breathed a half sigh, never sure if of relief or disappointment that she wasn't yet 'with child.' Charles never asked.

He must be conscious of it. So could it be that he too realises that talking about it will change nothing?

She decided to let more water flow under their bridge before raising it.

There was little change out of living expenses. Accommodation and food was found, and Charles received work clothes as well as summer and winter uniforms, dress parades, or rallies as some called them, being a regular part of RE routine. Cash in hand was modest, yet they lived comfortably enough—comfortably enough that was, with Martha serving up meals learned from her mother's frugal repasts. These were still much to Charles' tastes, however—such 'delights' as he called them, of cattle-tripe stewed in milk with healthy fistfuls of parsley in the pot, and 'pork belly-scrags' stewed with whatever root vegetables the itinerant hawker stocked.

We certainly eat better than if a man were scrounging for whatever work he could get in the city, Charles would sum up as he patted his thankful stomach after meals.

When the north Wales line became operational, Charles hoped more of his old unit would be transferred to Goole, that he and Richard would be together again. Yet the 'western unit' began work on a west-coast extension to Glasgow. Goole remained home base for surveying the line north to Edinburgh, with several branches to North Sea ports.

The further from Goole the team advanced, of course, made it a greater number of days before Charles could get 'home,' yet Martha happily found Annie a fine replacement for Julia's friendship. Not so deep, but satisfactory enough.

Annie had had her first babe since arriving, a girl, and by the time the team had been two years operating out of Goole, was expecting her second.

"Good company for me, in the circumstance, Charles," Martha had said when satisfied that she was, indeed, on the way with her first.

Whitgift had few facilities. Yet with so many household needs provided, army wives wanted for little when it came down to necessities. Annie had no more education than Martha, so Martha sorely missed the help Julia had been in respect of studies. Yet whilst she hadn't quite forsaken them, with Charles now away longer, she had made little progress with her reading.

I hadn't realised the convenience of having Julia handy. I'm now realising how many stumbling blocks there have ever been.

Yet Annie was a help when it came to cooking. Living in one's own home and fending for oneself in respect of cooking, housework, sewing, and knitting was a far cry from housekeeping at the Manor. Here Martha had to do for herself, so for Annie's experience in establishing routines and labour-saving shortcuts she was indeed thankful.

Yet now with a babe on the way, something getting close to the two-month mark, I expect I'll feel up to doing less and less.

She was at least thankful that in the bivouac there was no dairy work involved.

And Annie, she found, pulled no punches when it came to talking perversely freely about her 'private' life.

"We do it every night Arthur is home, you know," she told Martha. "It sometimes seems that the longer hours he's been working as days lengthen, he should be more tired, yet these are the times he seems more anxious to get to bed. But I don't mind. It's his right, I suppose. And we try so many different ways. Sometimes we're standing up, sometimes he's lying on me or I'm sitting on him. Sometimes it's doggy fashion. We try them all some nights—it makes it very hard on a girl when I'm trying the Rhythm Recipe so I don't fall again so soon."

Martha would try not to look shocked.

...Difficult when not only have I been taught never to discuss such things with anybody but my husband—even with him sometimes, Ma was ever telling me. And when any time women in the Manor kitchen discussed problems of things personal it was always nod and wink, with everything clouded in unsubtle hints. I've ever since my first curse, when Ma swore me to silence on all things so personal, taken care not to sound common... "Gossip-mongers will quickly label you hoyden," she would say.

Yet it was clear Annie was no hoyden. Annie had even told Martha she'd never had even a hint of anything physical with a man before marriage. "Even Arthur I kept at arm's length until the knot was tied," she had said, "so much so that the minute the door was closed behind us on our wedding night, he was feeling me here, squeezing me there, and making such funny wheezing sounds that I thought he was having trouble breathing."

~ * ~

Little Charles Frederick bawled his way into life the following September.

Annie had despatched a lad off on his bicycle for the midwife, yet by the time she arrived, having been attending another birth, it was all over bar congratulations. Annie had the babe all washed and swaddled and was trying to clean up the bed best she could, alone. She had been anxious to lay the boy in Martha's arms, a Martha still offering silent prayers of thanks that the birth, despite painful enough to make her wonder if she should want another, left her with no dwindling pain.

"Easier than poppin' pimples, it was," the artless Annie told the midwife.

Martha made no comment yet smiled at the expression. She tucked it into the cranny of her mind so she could tell Charles.

This wasn't to be for a few days, so the midwife filled in the official notification form she drew from her satchel. She showed Martha where to sign.

"I shall hand it in to the registrar in Goole," she said.

Lying in the bed and trying to append the signature Charles had spent torturous hours having her practise made the task awkward indeed with the ink running backwards on to her fingers. The signature became little more than an unintelligible blob. So the two women hoisted Martha high enough that she could make another attempt.

"I'll make my mark," she said, accomplishing it in a fraction of the time she knew it would take to laboriously write such a long signature when propped up so uncomfortably.

"Having a baby in bed, Annie, is easier than trying to write a signature in bed."

She didn't realise her two carers of the moment were so chuffed at her comment that Annie stored it up to tell Charles. The midwife even reported it to the local weekly news. They published it the following Saturday.

"They made such a to-do about it, Charles," she said as two days later he strutted proudly about the room with his son in his arms, "as if I meant it seriously. But the thought had tickled my own mind so much, it just came out."

"Well I'm sure our son is as happy for you that the birth was not too difficult, as am I. You were in my mind, of course."

He held the baby low for her to see the contented smile on his little face.

"All little ones, even until several years old, look not only contented when asleep, Charles, but even angelic. Have you noticed that?"

And asked to consider it, he now realised he had.

He spent quite some hours that night writing letters to Mother Mary, Mother Sarah, sister Julia, and Uncle John.

"Maybe, Arthur," Charles said to his mate, "I could have finished the letters in half the time if you and Annie hadn't arrived with two bottles of beer."

"I would have brought more had I not known the girls wouldn't indulge. It comes as a relief to a man when he marries that his wife don't like beer. Do you feel the same, mate?"

Charles, in fact, thought it a shame Martha didn't like beer. He liked to share his beer when relaxing; it was a comfortable feeling. Martha would occasionally have a shandy, yet preferred her own lemonade. She made it whenever she could get the lemons.

"Home-made is always better than machine-made," she would insist.

She was quickly up and about after the birth.

"Not my style to be abed wanting people to fuss over me."

And with little Charles to tend, she felt even greater rapport with Annie—they began to spend even more time together.

"She is the most candid of persons," she would confide to Charles. She knew he wouldn't pass on to Arthur comment that could be misconstrued as mischief. "In many respects she reminds me of my father. 'Don't just come out with whatever is in your mind, William, without thought for propriety,' Ma would tell him. And Annie is like him in that. Yet I see an honesty about it, about being open."

"Society has rules, Mother." He had taken to calling her 'Mother' on occasions, and she enjoyed the touch.

"Some see conventions as sacrosanct—your own mother, for instance."

"And some see it as prudish, Charles. Surely there is room for latitude in people letting their own personalities show."

"Some call it 'a modern outlook.' You wouldn't want to try it in the army, girl, you'd be up on a charge of 'insubordination.' In the field we can get away with calling junior officers by their Christian names if we know them well, yet only in private. They'd be the first one to have us up on a charge if we did it in front of their seniors."

"Different people have different actions and different reactions in different situations, Charles, and I agree that circumstance must be taken into account. Papa doesn't take circumstance into account—he simply speaks his mind all the time. It's not a 'damn you if you don't like it' attitude, because he has no vindictive streak—he simply doesn't take convention into account. Like Annie. That is why she doesn't even think I might be offended. I see it a compliment of sorts, illustration that she feels so comfortable with me, that she can be herself."

"Arthur's like you in that. He takes it from Annie as a matter of course. He is frank with me, at times, although not in other company. The army teaches one to consider circumstance—there's only one way to do anything, in its book. They have everything categorised into a rule…

"…and 'their' book has precedent even over the Bible," he added with a grin.

Martha changed the subject.

"Your moustache is taking shape."

Ever since meeting her he had been trying to grow it, but he found it one of those things a man can't hurry. But it was happening at last.

She liked a man with hair on his chest, and her man had not too much, just enough to be attractive.

"You're lucky, Charles, that both your parents had black hair. Your ma told me your father was like that. My Burgess family all have dark hair, but the Billings are fair. That's why I'm like a mouse—never a satisfactory colour for a woman. But like your moustache growing, there's nothing I can do to make my hair grow black. It has its own mind."

"Your hair is just right. It fits you well, my darling."

"Then your mind is like the army's—different indeed from my Billing mind. But in this instance, my darling, let's just put it down to 'nicely conventional.'"

~ * ~

In the first year of the century's second half, two significant events happened in Charles' and Martha's lives.

Finally reaching the 'wilds' of Yorkshire was news of the impending opening of the first worldwide trade exhibition. For some years, since Britain had announced it would mount the world's first exhibition of quality engineering, manufacturing, art, and artefacts from as many countries in the world as cared to mount meaningful displays, work towards staging it had been in progress.

The Great Exhibition had triggered global interest, and naturally enough it was to be held in the world's largest city, which more than co-incidentally was capital of the world's most industrialised nation. Prince Albert himself accepted the presidency of the organising body, and an area of London's Hyde Park was set aside for building the most modern structure the world had ever seen. The *Crystal Palace*, as the mammoth steel and glass edifice became known, was indeed revolutionary architecture, in itself a marvel of the industrial revolution.

Outwardly, its huge proportions projected drama with astounding impact, and inside, halls and courts were designed for displaying every art, science, history, and culture from all corners of the globe.

At about the same time as news of the opening reached Goole, Charles' Survey Corps unit announced it was transferring from Yorkshire to Scotland's Glasgow.

Charles clapped his hands.

"What an ideal time to take advantage of the two-weeks leave I've accumulated! How would you like it if we went up to London to take in the Great Exhibition?"

Martha gasped.

"Ah! I have never really been anywhere. You mean we not only travel to London, Charles, and not only get to visit the Great Exhibition, but we stay in a hotel?"

"Compared to most English mothers, my dearest, you have travelled much of England and are about to move habitat to Scotland. Yet before we do, and the Corps has suggested that those of us wishing to take entitled leave should do so before taking up bivouac there, we should go to London. Should we not, we could regret the opportunity for the rest of our lives."

Martha had heard from army wives who could read that the Great Exhibition was planned to transport one, in her mind, to every corner of the world. It was indeed an opportunity to grasp.

"When, Charles? And we must take little Frederick."

They had decided to call little Charles Frederick, Frederick. It would have proved decidedly confusing to have both father and son called Charles.

"I have broken family convention enough by not calling him William, my love," Charles had declared, "so I think it matters not a whit if we dub our boy Frederick after my dear brother."

"Well, we should call our next son, William," Martha had replied.

For Charles to rejoin with, "Indeed. Whether it be after your father or mine, my dear, we should not press each other for a response. But yes, indeed, William our next son must be."

Little Charles Frederick would ever be socially known as Frederick.

Anything is better than giving him a name like Allison, for instance!

"Let me check first with the staff sergeant, but we have licence to nominate any time within the two months prior to the Corps' move to Scotland. I feel we should time our journey to arrive in London not sooner than a week or three after the opening, which not only allows time for organisers to iron out glitches but avoids the stampedes of those who feel they must be first to get through the gate. What I also need do is check to see if His Majesty's Royal Engineers can make hotel bookings through some agency. I don't much like the idea of arriving in London without having booked. I would hate to see you and young Frederick having to jostle for sleeping space on a St. Pancras platform."

Martha felt excited enough to simply say 'yes' to anything, provided it meant better enjoying what would likely prove the greatest feature of a person's life.

Her tummy nerves trembled uncontrollably.

Oh! It will surely be the thrill of a lifetime.

Eleven

In London's Shoreditch, Ed and Maggie Bourn, whilst Ed's career had taken off with a bang once settling into his role as Design Manager at Wright Brother's Battersea plant, had had a less successful and hence unhappy family side to their lives.

It was fortunate, with Ed spending such long days at the plant, that Mother Martha Rawes lived with them. Maggie had been desperately ill leading up to her first confinement and their baby, a daughter, died before having lived even a week. The death was put down to 'unknown causes,' and Maggie's illness lingered. The Rawes family doctor, a Harley Street man of several years' repute, thought her condition spleen-based. Another thought it more likely the colon. The ruptured appendix fear, a fatal affliction, was crossed off the list of highly possible causes only when Maggie continued to live longer than such an affliction had ever allowed.

"A substance called ether has recently been demonstrated in America," the Bourns were told. "It dulls a patient's sense of feeling to such an extent that surgery can be performed while the patient is comatose. The patient feels nothing until awakened after the wound has been stitched and dressed. Several Harley street physicians are currently in the United States establishing details."

Ed was distressed at the thought of deliberately cutting into people with a knife whilst still alive. He couldn't imagine such a thing without the patient knowing and suffering the pain.

"However it will likely be months before trials on animals can be conducted here," the doctors insisted, "so many months that exploratory surgery cannot help your wife."

It was a feeling of utter helplessness—and no consolation at all was the realisation that millions of people around the world must be in as helpless a situation.

Medicines helped, but Maggie never reached the stage of feeling the problem was overcome. A year after the baby's death, she fell pregnant again. Every caution was taken that she have the best chance of a successful birth. Yet when little Edward was born and had, for his first two months seemed to be thriving, he had suddenly sickened and died. So was it fear more than joy, that the family felt when Maggie was reported pregnant a third time?

"It's too soon, Ed," she told him. "I cannot believe I have conceived again so soon. There must be another answer."

Yet the doctors were proved correct. So it was back to bed for Maggie, to rest until the baby was born. And still it came early. Ten months after the birth of little Edward, Maggie gave birth to a tiny but fully developed baby girl they named Rose Ann.

And the tot, quickly dubbed Rosa, thrived. It was Maggie's old condition that seemed to mysteriously die.

"It's uncanny, Ed. I can't help but be over-conscious of sensing the old illness returning, but no twinge develops."

They could only hope it would never return.

Three years later, the year of London's Great Exhibition, Jessie was born.

And after a further two years, Edith.

During those years Ed and Mother Rawes watched Maggie's confidence take more positive steps towards a full recovery. With now three healthy daughters and her vibrant energy returned, she progressively became, again, a happy woman.

"You look even younger than five years ago," Ed told her.

"And feel it, my dear. I had come to believe I was never going to recover. My only joy in those times was realising that you were enjoying your work, that your promotions were proving accomplishments whilst I was denying you others."

"Never, my dear. Although I now can say that I had to try extremely hard not to let you see how stressed I was at being able to do no more than keeping your spirits up. Your mother and I were both in that unhappy state. It was a sense of hopelessness to be sure."

Edward Bourn's work had earned him a considerable number of accolades. He was the company's chief designer and had earned particular repute for his adventurous approach in respect of luxury first class carriages. Using the best of continental as well as local fabrics in the form of leathers and suedes, mohair, and velvets, he as well added sophisticated upholstery techniques that had never before appeared in vehicles of transport. His first-class carriages were now fitted with not only traditional studded cushioning for all seats, but using the new coil springs. He never stinted in choices of drapes and blinds, nor for lamp sconces and furniture, even for public use, let alone in fulfilling requirements for Royal carriages.

"It goes further than the gloss, however," he would remark of his duties. "The techniques of designing machinery that our standard carriages can accommodate many different-sized bogies, is a design art in itself. And the longer our tracks extend through the kingdom, there is even, now, a need for dining cars on major lines—with entire kitchens aboard."

However, when Edie was but a year old, Mother Rawes died. They buried her with her Gerard in St. John the Baptist's churchyard.

"Papa will be happier now she is with him again," Maggie said as they walked home.

"I can never forget during my growing up years, that while all my friends would talk about the quarrels their parents frequently had, mine never did. At least I was never witness to any."

"It was his second marriage, of course; and your ma had lived with your pa and his first wife for many years, wasn't it?"

"Yes. Papa and his Mary lived a social life. Mama, ostensibly hired as Mary's 'companion' became, as well, tutor to the children. I think that's the way it was. So she was sort of Nanny to them too. She and Papa married a year after Mary died bearing James. Mama became stepmother to all three, to then have Francis, then me. There was a third, but she died as a babe."

"An interesting life. And a studious one, it has been patently obvious."

"She was a great reader of classics as well as a competent teacher. And they travelled once we were grown, to the Balkans. We were fortunate children."

~ * ~

Edward Bourn was called to a boardroom meeting. It had already been some hours in progress.

"Let's get this bit of business out of the way quickly so we can get to the heart of what we want to talk about," was the chairman's opening statement.

Ed realised, because of the hour, that financial matters would have by now been dealt with, and that they were up to current business proposals.

So the matter at hand, it would seem, is to do with my responsibilities?

Under the table, he crossed the fingers of both hands.

"There is a vacancy on the board, and we are desirous of appointing an additional director. Are you prepared to fill that vacancy?"

Bloody hell. I know my hearing is not impaired. But surely they have more mature men here or in the Birmingham works. Why should they approach me?

The silence of every man at the table, staring at him, lords and knights included, was shooting excruciating pains through his entire system.

His first words were inaudible, even to him.

"I... I am, sir."

"All in favour?"

Forefingers of all were raised.

"Great. Welcome aboard, lad. Now… this special project you've been responsible for during the past year, the coaches for New South Wales, is nearing completion?"

He nodded. *So is this about my next project?*

"You will also realise that once these coaches arrive in the colony, there is a five- to six-month turn-around in communications should there be problems?"

He nodded.

"The NSW government will not be prepared to flit away five or six months when they have stock ready to roll. You appreciate that?"

"Of course. It is common sense."

The chairman almost let his scowl become noticeable.

Oh-Oh. That last sentence was utterly needless. Every man around this table recognises that my 'Of course' adequately answered the question. Or could that old codger down the deep-end of the table nearly nodding off, be an exception?

"Our man on the spot must have ability, responsibility, and authority to make decisions at the moment. Agreed?"

"Yes, sir." *Am I right in thinking where all this is leading?*

"You, Bourn, have the best ability available. Now a director, you have additional responsibility to our shareholders. For you to be our man in the colony of New South Wales, he with the most knowledge of the engineering facets and values of all nine carriages and capacity as advisor to their further requirements, is our collective opinion. You lack only authority. Are you beginning to understand our situation?"

He drew in a deep and obvious breath.

I have to transport Maggie and our daughters from the only sort of home they've ever known, Maggie having grown up with every family comfort at her fingertips, used to servants fulfilling every household need, to endure colonial life?

His mind flashed through what he had heard about Australia—a rough and hostile land with few comforts, yet a land with opportunity aplenty, being rich in wool and beef and minerals. It was the only colony already milling its own steel for rail-lines and seemed to find buried under its deserts inexhaustible supplies of both coal and iron ore. And Newcastle to where the carriages were destined, for rail lines north from Sydney, was a coal-mining town with yet few comforts...

He was interrupted by a cough from the chair.

Am I thinking where all this could be leading? I sure as hell am! But am I committing if I say 'yes'?

"Yes, sir."

"We cannot ensure against the massive losses that incur if spare parts, other than those despatched with the carriages, cannot be made in New South Wales. If they have to be made or repaired here it can mean a twelve-month turn-around—quite unacceptable. We can only place in you, Bourn, our trust that you are prepared to undertake, before shipment, both human and inhuman measures to ensure the carriages, spare parts, and tooling equipment you take with you, will give twelve months trouble-free service from the time the carriages begin rolling. That gives you no more than three months to assess local conditions in respect of what tooling and engineering skills are available. You will select four of our engineers to accompany you, for either those three months assessing, or to remain with you with a view to local manufacture. How does all that sound, eh?"

Thoughts continued rolling around his mind like a kaleidoscope...

At least with my own technical expertise to hand, I won't be alone in any dilemmas. Yet I expect local facilities are poor in the extreme. And any that there are, only in Sydney—and there is yet no rail link between Sydney and Newcastle—everything must travel by sea.

They were, he was aware, still trying to find a route over the mountains north of Sydney for a road, let alone a railroad.

He heard another cough.

"It sounds fine, sir. I shall start tomorrow, selecting men, shoring up quality inspection weaknesses, and working on what spares should be taken."

The chairman smiled as several of the directors put hands together for a quiet little clap.

"Why wait until tomorrow, Bourn? You've a half hour before tonight's whistle blows."

Quiet giggles reached his ears, but the message was clear.

"Any questions for Director Bourn?" the chairman asked.

Informal questions, answers, and suggestions were then, for the next hour, tossed around the table. No one turned a hair when the night whistle sounded, other than the secretary closing her notebook and opening the bar cupboards so the directors could help themselves.

~ * ~

In order to be closer to the plant for the eighteen months before shipping, Ed moved his family from Shoreditch to Battersea Fields. The company paid for the staff required to move the largely pregnant Maggie and all the Bourn household to their temporary Battersea lodgings—large and old, but comfortable.

"That road tunnel under the Thames, my dear, through which we transported our possessions," Ed said to her, "has long tended my mind to thinking something quite revolutionary. I am certain, in my mind, that one day railways shall travel not only via fields and riversides, but under cities—via such tunnels. Can you imagine, for instance, railway lines travelling beneath the city of London? I find it an absolutely challenging prospect."

Maggie frowned deeply.

What a startling revelation! Not trains in tunnels, of course, but that my Ed shows a twist to humour I've never before recognised.

So she dismissed the frivolous incident completely from her mind.

And then three weeks later, she presented him with their fourth daughter, Eliza.

Twelve

"Come on, Mother, I'll help you up."

Martha couldn't recall feeling so cumbersome when carrying Frederick.

"I'm sure I have twins in here."

"Big and bonny ones."

They were boarding the train in Goole. Their every possession was stowed in the luggage van. Annie was near as large, and Arthur had already spread his hands across her broad buttocks to wedge her up and through the doorway.

Their entire unit was moving to Glasgow.

When, several months prior, Charles had gone to the staff sergeant to apply for leave in London, there was no trouble having it dated from the third week of The Great Exhibition opening. And there was a choice of recommended hotels for army personnel. He chose one in a modest price bracket and was assured that whilst it was not close to the exhibition, it was right by a train station on a direct line to Hyde Park.

"Maybe it's a reasonable price, Mother, because it's by the railway line. However, we cannot be choosy because it's the one the RE recommends."

Martha wasn't choosy. If it were so easy getting to the Exhibition, it would suffice.

They had known for a time that she was again expecting, but nothing was going to deter her from seeing London. The excitement of preparing for it was like a dream coming true. So she soon found herself clickety-clacking all the way to it. She not only saw much countryside but had bird's-eye views of the several cities between. Both felt guilty passing through Kettering—so close to Northampton City, Brington, and Brixworth. Yet to visit family in all three would have robbed them of touring not only London city but the delights promised by the Exhibition.

"Maybe you can stop off with the boy, on the return journey," Charles suggested. "I will need to get back, but you can visit the families."

Martha had put that thought into the back of her mind.

Let's see how tired I feel after London. If it's as big as they say, and I'll want to see Buckingham Palace, Piccadilly Circus, St. Paul's Cathedral, and oh, simply so many other places...

The Great Exhibition was remaining open for five long months so as many people as possible could see it. It was promoted as so big that in an entire day it was impossible to take in more than a little of what it contained; and there would be much to tantalise hungry eyes and minds. Charles had purchased five-day passes.

The entire journey indeed proved a wakeful dream for both. Martha found herself in raptures, her mind transported on Persian and Turkish carpets to exotic temples of ancient Greece, Egypt, and Babylon; to European museums of Renaissance painters and sculptors; and to such exotic lands as China and India.

The Exhibition proved a masterpiece of promotion for England and the thrill of a lifetime for Martha.

And now they were saying farewell to Yorkshire and heading for the further adventure of Scotland.

~ * ~

When Frederick was two, Martha gave Charles a second son, William Arthur, the William a tribute to both their fathers and

Arthur after the child's godfather. Arthur and Annie had asked to be godparents and were readily accepted.

"And we'll do the same for you, Annie," they promised.

So it had not been twins, merely an extremely large baby that meant a more difficult birth than her first...

...Yet tolerable. I was not looking forward to two tiny babies to care for.

The next three years proved pretty much the same sort of life they had enjoyed in Whitgift except that for Martha home was in a large city rather than a quiet fishing village.

And she quite disliked Glasgow.

Every building of dark grey stone robs the city of prettiness. It is all so sombre. And the sky seems forever overcast and threatening.

She found the summers short, autumn too eager to rush into winter, and winter seeming loathe to make way for spring.

"It's not a welcoming place, Charles. The bitter winds off the Atlantic keep it so cold. I heartily wish that one day when you arrive home you will tell me we must move again."

"If we are moved, Mother, it will be further north. The line is to extend to Wick and Thurso—right up by John O'Groats, which they say is the windiest place in the world."

Martha shuddered. Their immediate future looked less inviting than at any time since marrying. Suddenly, she realised with a shock, for the first time she was missing Brixworth.

Yet guilt wags its finger at me when I have such thoughts...

She looked at her two little ones sound asleep.

If I were still the Manor's housekeeper back in Brixworth, look what I'd have missed...

~ * ~

Yet the day arrived when she was rescued from the dilemma of moving closer to the North Pole. Three years after little William was born, when six months into her third pregnancy, reprieve from her present sentence arrived. Charles came home from a field trip with startling news.

"Prepare yourself for a shock, mother of two, or should that be of two-and-a-half?" he joked. "I have made a momentous decision on our future. It will set us up nicely for a considerable time as well as offer adventure."

She sat waiting, almost a-tremble.

What on earth has he committed me to?

Her mind flew to John O'Groats, blistering winds, snow and ice.

But she had not long to wait for the answer.

"The Corps is to survey the entire colony of Van Diemen's Land as a matter of priority. We are well advanced with our work here, and seven volunteers were called for, to ship to the great south land."

Martha's heart heaved.

Oh yes, I longed for news of quitting Glasgow. But Van Diemen's Land?

All she knew of it was that it lay at the extremity of the world, a penal colony with a fearful reputation. She could not speak. She was utterly stunned, her throat seizing up.

"Regimental surveyors are already there, but short of numbers, Mother. They need a further seven of us."

Her mind was racing—so many thoughts fought for pride of place...

"Can the Corps force us? They don't own us, Charles—it's not as if we are their slaves. And people say it is a cruel place—and on the other side of the world where it is very hot?"

"No, Mother, they cannot force us. They called for volunteers, and we lads put our heads together overnight and decided to go. We volunteered—seven of us. Seven who are not looking forward to field-work in Scotland's frozen north."

"But the convicts, Charles?"

"Not any more, Mother. They told us two years ago that England agreed to colony requests that no more convicts will be sent to Australian shores. Things are changing there. Van Diemen's Land is even changing its very name that the convict past is the more quickly forgotten. Tasmania, it is to be called, a colony as free as is England. And I don't know about it being hot. It is well south."

"Where will we live, Charles? And we know nowt of that country. Do they speak English?"

"Of course they speak English, girl. It's English people who settled it. And they have the same money as us. And eat the same foods. In fact, according to the captain, they eat better. And also, mother of two-and-a-half, we not only get the same pay as here, I will as well receive a 'colonial allowance.' And at the end of my tenure, if we decide to stay, I get a 'settlement allowance.' Or we can return here."

Her mind was still racing.

"How much higher pay?"

"Regimental pay remains the same. I receive an extra sixpence a day Colonial Allowance and a shilling a day field allowance whether in the field or in bivouac. All keep for the family is found. We will be much better off, my girl."

"The children, Charles—the boys can come? And this one?" She patted her tummy.

"Of course the boys come. And a doctor will be aboard so you'll have constant care the entire journey. That's more than you get here, girl."

Martha didn't know about going all that way by ship. She knew people got sick aboard ship.

I'll be sick enough with the new babe—and ships sink in storms, and I can't swim. Must a woman simply watch her babies drown? And coping with the boys aboard ship?

Her mind flew to the active young Frederick racing about as he ever did, trying to clamber up the rigging after the seamen.

And little William still toddling? Oh dear!

But even as her hand flew to her mouth, she could see how excited Charles was. She knew he would not even want to retract—*even if the Corps would let him, now that he's signed. Yet he did say, "Or we can return here," so it's not as if we're being transported for the rest of life like the convicts.*

In one sense it was another instance of Charles taking a decision before she'd had any opportunity of offering an opinion on it... *Yet I have to concede that in every other, he has been proved right, that it was to our benefit. I just do wish, though, that sometimes it would be nice to have a say in things. But it's not a wife's prerogative, unfortunately, to do aught than follow.*

She valued family harmony too much to risk rocking the boat.

She was beginning to see, giving it further thought, that this particular move, despite such a momentous twist to their lives, a twist in every sense of needs, goals, and dreams, did seem to have advantages. Her mind, as practical as convention insisted she was allowed, began clearing away a few of the clouds that had so quickly enveloped the declaration.

"How long is your tenure, Charles?"

She needed to know her term of conviction.

"Depends how long the job takes, and we cannot know that until there. It can depend on many things, the terrain, the weather, the co-operation we get from authorities... How long? Maybe three years, four or even more? The early core went a year ago only to find, once begun, that they need reinforcements. Word is that all who went find the conditions hard but survivable. And there'll be other wives and children, so you won't be alone. Arthur and Annie will be along."

Martha began thinking about family. She had never known anything but living close by parents and grandparents, aunts and uncles and cousins.

Even Yorkshire and Scotland seemed so far from kin. And in Van Diemen's Land I will have none! If only I had a few letters to pen words, I'd at least be able to write home. Maybe Charles will have time, once on the ship, to teach me more. It will likely take some months. And this one in my belly? It will to be born at sea! But Charles did say there's a surgeon aboard.

Her days of worrying about how she might cope when moving around Britain with the Corps, returned.

But there can no longer be the valve in my loneliness of taking a train back to Northampton. I might as well be now setting off for the moon.

They were to sail with their two boys, on the ship *Conway*.

This Twist with a capital T in their lives, however, soared to highlight proportions when breaking their journey to Tilbury docks by stopping off for overnights in Northampton, Brixworth, and Brington. In saying goodbye to every family member, it was realised that each farewell was in every likelihood an admission they would never see any of them again...

"Every loving person we've ever known," they told each other, "is to become nowt more than something of our past."

A devastating realisation when put like that...

Such a twist was one neither had felt prepared for.

"And we'll never see a sight like that again," she said as the four took post from Brixworth, pointing up to the proud and unique All Saints. They had spent an hour walking through its graveyard paying respects to Bray, Burgess, and Richardson ancestors, and Martha's three little Joseph Billing brothers.

More than a thousand years old, Charles thought at his last glimpse of the church, *not only the largest Saxon building in the world, but oldest still servicing mankind—ah! Where we are going it's likely that for the rest of our lives we'll never see anything older than something built by today's fathers and grandfathers.*

The momentous changes their lives faced seemed more numerous at every turn.

Thirteen

The boys, at age five and three, had remained agog for days.

They had never seen a ship, let alone gone aboard one. Nor had they seen the sea.

Oh, what adventure lay ahead! Whilst the *Conway* was modestly sized and powered by steam as well as sail, to the boys it was a veritable galleon to excite even the blasé.

Martha was another who had seen neither ship nor ocean, yet as the conveyance to conduct them to the very antipodes it seemed exceedingly fragile. She admitted having no comparative measure, although she had certainly expected something more substantial. Her only sense of encouragement arose from, firstly, the fact that Charles illustrated no concern and secondly that other wives she knew, with their children, were either already aboard or still en-route. She looked forward to hearing their impressions.

How will we fare with fresh food for the boys? And being afloat for as many weeks as they say the journey will take, surely we must all experience sickness? And drinking water…

"Surely, Charles, after so many weeks, it must be brackish. I don't want brackish water fed to my boys. There is danger of cholera."

"These people have centuries of experience in keeping people healthy on voyages, girl. England is the greatest seafaring nation on earth, so they know what they're about. Have faith, my dear. There is a galley aboard, and maybe the cook will welcome some assistance from you wives if you make yourselves known there. There you can enquire about the water being boiled, and you may even venture some input as to what is to be served up to us."

He smiled a devilish grin, as he said that.

Martha would wait, however. Yet she would maintain the teasing ambivalence of her thoughts until finished unpacking and storing their all. There was little space in their tiny cabin for all they'd surely need during the voyage.

When finished here, I will indeed make a tour of inspection—seek out the galley. I shall take Annie with me so we can together see what the cook has in store.

They steamed from Tilbury docks on a gloriously sunny day in late September, a decidedly crispy wind reminding all aboard that they were quitting the start of a northern winter.

"By the time we arrive, Mother, it will be an Australian summer."

Huh. All right for him to be thinking of nowt but what awaits us. I'm still concerned with what getting there has in store.

~ * ~

What Charles and his fellow surveyors remained unaware of, in relation to what awaited them, was the situation of the Corps' surveyors already at their destination.

Huge gold discoveries had been made in Victoria in 1851, which led to a flight of labour from Van Diemen's Land—enough to dislocate the entire fiscal stability of the colony. Governor Denison, himself an old RE man, dissatisfied with surveying results by contract surveyors whose work was now not being supervised, renewed an earlier appeal that had been denied. It was for a subaltern officer of the Royal Engineers and a small party of Sappers and Miners to assist in carrying out a trigonometrical survey. It was this time approved. Captain John Hawkins, RE, withdrew fifteen men from the Ordnance Survey of Great Britain, all volunteers. They were to be given the opportunity, should they wish to be discharged at the end of their labours, of settling in the colony. That party had reached Hobart Town four years before the *Conway* contingent set sail.

Hawkins arrived to find that Governor Denison had been transferred to the colony of New South Wales and that there was no programme in place in Van Diemen's Land for setting about what they had come for. Most severe pressure on the department, he found, was no longer the trigonometrical survey, but the survey of land selected under earlier regulations. All the contract as well as departmental surveyors employed on it had joined the gold-rush across the strait. The Sappers and Miners, therefore, were dispersed in twos or threes all over the settled parts of the island—an area greater than all of England.

Almost from the start, it seemed, the surveyors were the recipients of criticism from opposition benches. Within a year they had been the subject of three hostile motions, newspapers taking their cue from disgruntled politicians. The Sappers and Miners, however, enjoyed the support of both the government benches and the governor's office.

Both the surveyor-general and his deputy were with the opposition on the stalemate. They were not prepared to agree that the retention of the Sappers and Miners was essential to the efficiency of the department or that competent civil surveyors could not be procured.

"Every opportunity should be offered to local young men to enter this useful and honourable profession," they claimed. "The Sappers and Miners should not interfere with employment within the colony. To retain them will damage education and ambition."

In specific reference to the officers and seven Sappers and Miners and their families in transit per *Conway*, it was decided that the contingent *"should not be retained in the Survey Department longer than it will take to replace them with Civil Surveyors."*

The governor had no option but to relent. He approved the recommendation.

~ * ~

Aboard *Conway*, Charles stood at the rail while Martha reclined in the ship's only lounge-chair. They had chosen an 'open rail' so she could also enjoy the magical sight of a full moon glancing on what seemed an entire ocean-full of dancing ripples. They were drinking in the warm, salt-tanged air of the South Atlantic, Charles enjoying his habitual after-dinner pipe and Martha relaxing her roundly burdened body, thankful that the sea was so gentle.

Her third child was due 'any minute,' she had been warning him for the past several days. What he was not warned of, of course, was the sorry news awaiting the Corps members when arriving in Hobart.

He was disturbed instead, by Martha reaching up to grab his arm.

"Oh-oh, my dear. Please help me up—have someone summon the surgeon, then get me to my bed."

She gave birth to little Annie that very night.

~ * ~

Conway never berthed in Van Diemen's Land.

After four months afloat, having been delayed in war-torn South Africa for obscure reasons to do with its war, the 'relief delegation' of surveyors instead arrived in Tasmania. Whilst *Conway* was delayed in Cape Town, on the dawning of the New Year 1856, the colony of Van Diemen's Land changed its name in the hope that it would the more quickly lose its stigma of a land of horror.

It changed its name to Tasmania, and Van Diemen's Land was no more.

So it was in Hobart, Tasmania, that the RE contingent arrived, to find it bathed, as if in celebration, in the glorious greens and golds of Australia's wattle-trees in high summer.

Having come at the specific request of their fellow surveyors to fill a badly needed gap in the settlement's surveying skills, the contingent was expecting a rousing welcome from incumbent Sappers and Miners—but the dock was empty. Not even Captain Hawkins was there to meet them.

"He is currently in Sydney," they were told, "in consultation with the governor there. If his negotiations prove successful, all our surveyors, including you chaps and your families, will be transferring to New South Wales."

The outline of the history regarding the surveys was given them, along with the explanation that the captain was convinced that the 'in-house' wrangling in the colony's politics promised no secure future for the RE. He believed that Governor Denison in Sydney would have a more receptive ear than the beleaguered Governor of Tasmania.

And so it proved.

Captain Hawkins returned, to recall all S&Ms from the field.

"We all go to New South Wales," he informed his now twenty-two men and their families.

"That colony has, as yet, only a single rail line from Sydney Town, the twenty miles to the town of Parramatta. Surveying of lines north and west of Sydney is urgently required. The skills of our new arrivals will be of immense assistance in this regard."

"So it's to be 'home-from-home' work for us new arrivals, my dear," a happy Charles informed Martha, "surveying railroads. And for you, my darling mother of three, proving so wonderfully clever during the journey as to give me a bonny bouncing daughter who will hopefully grow just like her dear mama, Sydney Town is a far more advanced settlement than Hobart. With vast deposits of gold having recently been discovered in its west, a rail-line is needed there urgently."

So the dour atmosphere of their arrival was suddenly somersaulted into hope—that of achieving what Tasmania was unable to deliver.

"We leave within three weeks," they were told.

Martha didn't at all mind that they had more sailing to do. This time it was only a handful of days, and she had become totally absorbed in the excitement of arrival. Among the early consignment of REs was an only wife, highly delighted to discover four wives and several children off the *Conway*.

"I've felt so much alone," she told them. "I've now been told that in New South Wales, the entire RE Survey Ordinance is to bivouac in Parramatta and that married men will have separate bungalows as in the old country. So we will be our own little community."

Such news pleased Martha no end. "It will be up to us, now, Annie, to prevail on our respective husbands to ensure you and me are assigned neighbouring bungalows."

A nod and a wink sealed that agreement.

On boarding the SS *Tasmania* early in February, Captain Hawkins announced to his Corps that he had been appointed the first commissioner for New South Wales Railways—an honour indeed.

The gloom into which Charles and Martha had arrived was suddenly lifted.

Even the SS *Tasmania,* small as it was, first vessel to ever carry the new name, was new. She was indeed small, yet carried no sail.

"Totally steam-powered it is, Mother. It is an iron screw, rather than wind, that will convey you, me, and our children to our new life."

An Epic Life

BOOK 2

New South Wales

Fourteen

As the Richardson family sailed towards Sydney, Maggie Bourn in London was arranging the packing of their household goods while Ed oversaw the loading aboard two ships of nine carriages, three first-class and six second-class.

"And the spare parts, my dear," he told her, "seem almost as sizeable a consignment as the carriages."

He was using two ships so that if one should founder, all was not lost, a fact to make Maggie smile inside.

I shan't question him now, on why his precious cargo is being despatched aboard two ships for safety, while his entire family is to sail in only one. I shall save that up until after we've arrived.

She could see the gross impracticality of splitting the family, of course, yet was highly amused when comparing the parallels. However, she found nothing amusing in being uprooted from her familiarly comfortable life, to take up one heavily burdened with unknowns.

Had Mama remained alive, of course, it would have been traumatic had she not wanted to come. My only really close kin are Francis and Caroline. It seems sad having to class stepsiblings as 'not so close,' but then, too, had Papa still been alive, it would have made that side of my family closer. But I have no option but to make the best of going to Australia. Trying to classify who I will miss most is entirely counter-productive.

Of course I will miss much. But I must concentrate on realising it is fate that takes me so far away. At least the journey will be comfortable. Ed inspected the first-class apartment when arranging the loading of the carriages and lauds its comforts. It even has a cubicle off our private nursery, for Nanny.

Wright Brothers' other employees were travelling second class.

"An advantage, however," Ed told her, "is that the dining room for first and second class is common, which will make it easier for us to fraternise during the journey. It is imperative that I don't create too much of a gap between me and those I am so dependent on."

Maggie was eight months 'along the way' with a new baby when they sailed. She had, fortunately, since the loss of her first two, next to no problems either carrying or bearing the next four, so she at least faced the looming birth aboard with confidence. Had she harboured any particular disappointment in respect of losing her first two it was that one had been a boy—the only boy of the six offspring she had so far borne.

Ed was so excited then—insisting we name him Edward; yet each time since, I've disappointed him.

She could only hope the one she now carried would be a boy.

"What do we do about registering births aboard, Ed? Will he be English or New South Welsh?"

"I'm told that in some lands the birth is registered at the ship's next port of call, in which case it would be Cape Town. Yet British ships travelling to British colonies tend not to present relevant papers until arrived in whichever colony. I am inclined to think our next child will be considered New South Welsh. But you can ask the captain. We are to dine at his table every night."

The usual round of farewells was made in London and Canterbury where Ed had grown up, with appropriate tears and promises to keep in touch by mail, and wishes for continued health and happiness in their new lives.

Maggie sighed at the end of the round. "I don't want to be sounding selfish, or even unkind to so many kin, Ed, but I am so glad the farewells are over. The ones it seems hardest to find words for are the aunts—especially when they seem so inclined to blame us for causing such heartache."

He smiled. "I know what you mean. I find, however, the most tedious are parents of reluctant children, insisting I pick them up and smother them with kisses when few of the little blighters aren't even sure who I am—let alone care."

Maggie laughed outright. "Well, now I know that you too are happy to have all that behind us. We can now concentrate on making best endeavours at seizing a future, without feelings of guilt."

All signs indicated that neither would spend much time being concerned over leaving a London of hansom cabs, bustles, and stovepipe hats for whatever the colonies might offer in lieu. They more concentrated on the living realities of who they were taking with them rather than on those being left behind—four daughters aged five through two: Rosa, Jessie, Edith Mary, and Eliza Bristow...

...and he or she waiting to make itself known some time during the voyage.

~ * ~

The euphoria of the opening, less than a year ago, of the twenty-mile railway from Sydney to Parramatta had hardly waned when the Royal Engineers Corps of Sappers and Miners rode it to their new home.

Parramatta was a bustling town, named for its Aboriginal inhabitants long decimated. George Street held the local market, the little church where Annie was baptised immediately on arrival, and the largest building, all of clapboard, known as the Town Hall. What were now warehouses and meeting halls had been both the colony's sinister male-convict prison and what had generally been called The Female Factory. Across from them were stores purveying all that the local community required, from produce to foodstuffs and ladies' fashions. Behind George Street was a street of eminent houses, homes of gentry, and behind those, in turn, were homes vacated by convict prison officials. These were now assigned as bivouac residences of married Royal Engineers and families.

Martha had suffered pangs of absolute anguish as Annie was baptised in Parramatta's only church, her mind in distant All Saints. That trauma was compensated for, however, by their accommodation quarters—absolute luxury when likened to what Whitgift and Glasgow had offered. On discovering it, Martha felt not only immediately more at ease in her new world, but pampered.

"Benefit of the present governor being an ex RE general, my dear," Charles explained. "Captain Hawkins arranged it with him."

And when the opportunity of meeting that gentleman arrived she was quick to thank the Captain for engineering such benefits for his people.

~ * ~

'Railway' was one of the 'meaningful' words typifying the 'new' New South Wales image. Now freed of its convict yoke, people were anxious to embrace any concept illuminating a sense of 'deliverance;' all things new became, contrived or not, symbolic of 'the new image.' There seemed almost a fervour amongst the women of the community, Martha and Annie were agreed, even among those who had been convicts, to encourage every means of 'smothering' evidence of the colony's past.

'A meaningful contribution' became the byword attached to all things innovative.

The Parramatta railway was 'meaningful' indeed, clear illustration that what had been considered an outback community was 'outback' no longer. The town was clearly linked to the parent city Sydney by an umbilical cord of steel lines. The outback had been despatched further westward.

Treasury grants were already approved for lines south to Goulburn and north up the Hunter River from Newcastle; in the far north, domestic rail services were planned for the new settlement of Brisbane. Captain Hawkins was quick to announce, hoping word would quickly get back to the still fumbling Tasmanian survey teams, that the surveyors he had brought to New South Wales had even developed and built their own surveying equipment to broaden the gamut of that brought from England.

RE members became so well considered that he encouraged them to wear uniforms when abroad in the town on even personal engagements. And when walking out with their men, Martha, Annie, and other wives did so with chins just a mite higher than they had ever done 'back home.'

"I'm fast coming to like this place, dear," Martha remarked to Charles one evening. "There is a togetherness here that Glasgow lacked, a sense of achieving—something never evident there. Things here happen quickly for the public good. It is indeed a comforting feeling."

"Well, that pleases me no end, my dear, that you feel it too. In the Corps we are also conscious of it. We believe it is because lines of decision-making are shorter than back home. Here questions can be asked directly of the highest authority in the land. Here, 'going through channels' is accomplished in a single conversation. That will change in time, for I have just learned that we are being sorted into operating units. Priority is being given to finding ways over the hurdles of mountains and rivers west and north, natural barriers that have defeated government explorers. I have been assigned to the Western Sector. We are back to field-work."

"Who are 'we,' Charles?"

"The Conway Seven. It seems a name dubbed that has caught the imagination of those in control here. Arthur, Walter, Tom, Tim, Martin, Henry and me. Word followed us from the old country that we have illustrated a worthy 'notch' in teamwork. The rest are assigned to the northern route, the quicker to find a route through the rugged mountains between here and Newcastle."

"And what of your 'Western Sector'? What do you yet know of it?"

"Huge deposits of gold have been found at Bathurst, the only real town west of the Blue Mountains. The road down the western side of the range is so precipitous as to be dangerous for both coaches and cargo-drays. A railroad is essential, yet so far, two search parties have failed, after months of back-tracking, to find a path through the maze of mountain valleys. We are told we must find a path that does not require tunnels."

"Why so? There are many tunnels in England."

"Aye, girl. But tunnels not only take forever to build but are prohibitively expensive. There are many rivers in the valleys of these Blue Mountains, and somewhere there is likely a connecting valley suitable for a line without every time finding high walls of granite. We've been commissioned to find it."

~ * ~

Captain Hawkins announced the new pay structure agreed with the surveyor-general. Charles' working pay would be five and sixpence per day, regimental pay one and tuppence-halfpenny, colonial allowance sixpence, and field allowance a shilling. He would receive rations, fuel, and quarters for his family and rations for himself when in the field.

"On eight and tuppence-ha'penny, Mother, we'll live comfortably indeed. It's a shilling more than in the old country."

Martha waited while he sat with pencil and paper and did the sums. His grin broadened as he sat up straight.

She felt so proud for him. *And he looks even more handsome with his moustache now thick and twirled at the ends...*

"One hundred and forty-nine pounds, two and sixpence ha'penny a year, Mother, with all keep found. Never did I imagine we could be so well off."

He re-worked the figures and wrote out a copy for Arthur.

"Arthur's the best mate a man could have, Mother, with many strong points, but arithmetic isn't one."

And he had a further piece of advice for her. "While we're away," he said in what he hoped sounded like an off-hand manner, "there's things you can do for other wives. They've all had the same experiences as you since leaving the old country, but none, girl, has your 'get-up-and-go.' They remain simply ready to follow their men. You are going to find, in this strange land, problems you didn't have back home. There is no backup here, of wives and children being thought about.

You must start seeking co-operation from authorities reluctant to think on matters we took for granted back there. So your friends, girl, will be looking for a leader, someone to turn the wheels."

She knew that when he called her 'girl' it was when the subject was of deep concern to him. She had learned to take particular heed when her man's serious side wanted to show itself.

"Will you be away longer here than back home?"

To her mind, the Corps was the Corps and lived by its same rules.

"The other unit is to first survey a line from here to Windsor, which will be home base for supplies to the 'Macquarie Towns' along the Hawkesbury River, and then on to Richmond. All the terrain along that area is known and pretty much a plains area before reaching the mountains. The road to the west is well travelled, but elevated. It quickly rises, west of here, to follow the ridges before dropping sharply down the western scarp. From there west, the country is as flat as a bloody billiard table, so they say. But a railway could never cope with the scarp getting down. So it's a path through the valley floors we must find—a goal so far having defeated three attempts."

"In Scotland, I recall you saying you went around a mountain, that was cheaper than cutting a tunnel?"

"This is not an isolated range. From the northern tip of this huge land, a mountain range runs the entire distance north to south, three thousand miles of it, all within a hundred miles of the east coast. It is not a high range, although due west of us here, for a long way north and south, the section called the Blue Mountains has stone walls that are perpendicular. Seeking a way through to the western plains, every water-course that has been followed seems to turn on itself—finds a way to empty eastward again."

"Well, how was the road built?"

"With twists and turns called 'hair-pins,' too sharp for a train-line. Thousand of them. All right for horses and wagons, except that in winter they must use bullocks because of the mud on such steep inclines."

"And if you cannot find a path at 'floor' level?"

"S and M's don't admit defeat, girl. We've to simply stay on the job until finding a path. The entire valley area is called The Grose. It is so much a maze, according to exploration reports, that some have said it can never get properly explored."

Martha was by now beginning to understand the wives could be being left to their own resources for extremely lengthy periods.

Fifteen

The early stage of the western line was easy to plot.

The twenty miles to the foot of the Blue Mountains was gently undulating.

The Conway Seven travelled by coach to Emu Plains, where a bridge spanned an upper reach of the mighty Hawkesbury River that flowed along the foothills.

"It's a hundred miles downstream of this very river that the Northern Sector team must find a route to where it can be spanned."

"Well, they're welcome to their problem, mates. Ours is the bloody Grose, and it can't be really as difficult as they claim."

It was well believed amongst surveyors that there was generally a way around difficult mountains. It was a case of searching every possibility on a trial and error basis.

"If we was bloody owls or eagles it wouldn't be difficult at all," Arthur bemoaned. "But foot-sloggers must do it the bloody hard way."

For the next three months, the Conway Seven sortied up valleys not previously explored. A fillip giving them fresh impetus was that, before striking out, they received notice from HQ that the S&Ms had been incorporated into the main RE category as fully-fledged engineers. New tabs declaring them such were issued for their uniforms.

Charles now realised why Captain Hawkins had given permission for full uniform to be worn in the street. "Henceforth," he declared, "we can strut even more proudly in full dress."

All realised the advantage of being seen on colonial streets in uniform. Here it was unique. Considerably more kudos was attached to uniforms than 'back home.'

However, they certainly were not in uniforms in the Grose Valley.

At the Parramatta market one day, Charles purchased a small volume entitled *Pocket History of New South Wales* and, being a newcomer, found it enlightening. He one day when 'on smoko,' pulled it from a pocket of his dungarees.

"Listen to this, mates," he said.

> *Major Francis Grose, Commanding Officer of the New South Corps, the marine division that relieved the First Fleet Marine Corps after its three year tenure:*
>
> *He was placed in charge of the entire settlement when Governor Phillip returned to England a sick man, until such time as a new Governor could arrive and that did not happen for a further two years. During that interim, Corps officers became exceeding rich at the expense of victimised settlers. Not only was the relieving Governor Hunter recalled 'for ineptitude' before his tenure was up, but Major Grose was recalled in 'damning disgrace.' When Governor Lachlan Macquarie arrived with his own 73rd Regiment of Foot Royal Highlanders, the entire New South Wales Corps was recalled on charges of 'gross negligence and corruption.' Most officers on arrival back in England immediately resigned in hopes of rescuing even a little of their career hopes.*

"So, mates, I find it surprising they haven't changed the name of this valley. Here was I thinking Major Grose must have been a pretty honourable sort of guy to have such a huge part of the country named after him."

His friends laughed. "Maybe they're waiting until the riddles of the valley are solved so they can name it after he who solves it?"

"What?" Arthur laughed with more than a hint of scorn. "Name it after one of us?"

Everybody laughed. But it was a nice thing to think on.

However, after their first week, nobody was laughing.

"It's a fair bugger, mates."

It was proving the 'utter maze' it had been described.

"Around every twist of the river we find another bloody wall of sandstone or granite."

"Well, we'll tomorrow have to backtrack and try the next tangent."

"Which will likely harbour more bloody mosquitos than this one."

"And in this one there are more than the one before it."

"Well, we've gotta keep goin.' We got an image to uphold."

And within a fortnight of Christmas, when returning to base with nowt to report but failures, they were told to head for home for a Christmas furlough.

In Sydney, the newspaper reported that politicians had raised, during the last session of the year, the high cost of supporting the Royal Engineers. Scant heed was given, it seemed, to the fact that three private expeditions had failed to find a path to the west. They concentrated only on the fact that if the RE could not find one, the colony was faced with the exorbitant cost of blasting two tunnels, the longest three miles through solid granite.

In February, Captain Hawkins released a report to the NSW Legislative Assembly detailing his unit's activities 'Up The Grose.' He distributed copies to his men.

"Hundreds of miles of levels we've taken, mates, in most-times deplorable conditions, to find acceptable gradients. What you reckon the pollies will make of that?"

"They'll simply want to know why it's taken so long. They've no interest in us fallin' arse first down rock ledges, diggin' bloody leeches out of our ankles from wadin' in the mire."

"It says here," Charles read from the tract, "the captain doesn't think it practicable to make use of the valleys of any stream here—that we have no recourse but tunnels through the elevated crags, no matter how much they cost."

"There's no way to get trains down that western scarp."

"A switch-back?"

"We've never surveyed a switch-back. And that would mean lots of excavating and shoring up edges. It would take an army of navvies."

"Why'd the colony abandon convictism? Convicts were all free labour," said Walter.

"Slave-labour," replied Tom.

Walter, Tom, Arthur, and Charles had become a foursome; they found common ground in thrashing out reasoned argument. Recognition of character strengths had developed, each appreciating the various ways of looking at contentious issues. And contentious issues were plentiful when enquiring minds were such essential engineering traits.

Come July, however, they were given leave for the first time in six months.

"Ah, a week home in Parramatta," they chorused.

~ * ~

Charles found Martha in high spirits.

They made frantic love, as if each had thought of nowt else during their long separation.

"There have been so many things happening, Charles. I never realised how children can occupy so much of a woman's time. All three are so active. The boys are forever running everywhere—they never just walk. Annie tries running after them. She doesn't seem to realise she'll only trip and fall again..."

"Which points to them all being healthy, Mother. And you're looking bonny yourself, with roses in your cheeks and eyes as bright as ever."

"Well, I'm feeling purposeful here, Charles, apart from the fact that it's becoming a pleasant place to enjoy. I've always lived a village life, and Parramatta life is much like that. Many new shops are opening, offering little things to improve life."

Charles smiled, not only because he could see she was adapting to the 'strangeness' of the local environment, but because her new thinking was running so parallel to his own.

"Know what the boys and I were discussing the other day, girl?"

"Now how could I?"

He laughed. "Right enough. We were then talking about these very things you just raised, although from a different angle—taking into account the differences involved when there are so few people in the land compared to back home. Back there, as villages grow, seems the first things they double up on are churches. When you count how many new buildings are being constructed, churches seem always on the list. Parramatta, when we came, had an only church. You yourself have just confirmed that many new buildings are being added to the town, yet there is still but the one church."

She thought on that.

"If you were to make that point to people back home, Charles, they would likely read into it that people here are not as church-minded. People here do still go to church."

"That's the point, girl. It's that there are more people in towns and villages, so one church would not be enough. But it doesn't alter the fact that on a 'per church' basis, we have more public or trading buildings than there, even though fewer people. We couldn't come up with an answer, but the figures speak for themselves."

They didn't to Martha. She was not comfortable with problems based on having to juggle figures around. She resorted to her usual answer to such difficulties, by changing the subject.

"I've been practising writing, Charles."

She showed him what she called her 'exercise book'—clear evidence of how early struggles developed, over several pages, from childish attempts to regular writing.

"And even running-writing, Charles."

She demonstrated how she'd developed a signature, to make him indeed proud for her.

"The signature, Mother, has to be something unique to you, something others can look on and recognise it as usual for you. It's important you don't let it vary."

"I know that. I looked at our marriage certificate and several other documents where you've signed—very elegantly too, and always much the same, even when put side by side."

"It has to remain so during your life."

"And there's something else I've been working on."

He waited.

She called the boys. Frederick was not 'little Frederick' any more. He was six-years old—"boy enough to make any father proud," Charles had told him when arriving home. William was four. Little Annie, forever at their heels, had met her father with her finger in her mouth.

"She's not sure of you, Charles."

He went to pick her up, but Martha stayed him.

"Watch this," she said.

She sat them all three down at table and gave each boy his exercise book, each with his name in bold letters on the cover. She gave Annie a slate and chalk.

"Show your pa what you can do," she instructed.

Charles could see that on each inside cover, Martha had lettered the entire alphabet in lower case. While Annie immediately began scribbling on her slate, Charles watched mesmerised as both boys began, on their next writing page, forming each letter.

"They're the only boys in all Parramatta getting schooling," she announced with a smile. "We work together. Annie will join us when a year or two older. There'll be no growing up without letters like I had to."

Then she returned to the subject of signatures. "I can recall always wondering about Mama's signature. I could never recognise any letter in it, yet it always looked the same."

"You don't have to be able to read it, Mother. It's still a mark in that respect—a mark illustrating that only you could be the one making it."

He kissed her, telling her how proud he was of her. Then he went to the bedroom.

"I brought some reading for you. They may prove difficult, but you can try—and put them aside until later if you want. I hadn't realised you were so well advanced, so maybe you can read them now—read them to

Annie. They are tracts we were given—histories of the Grose Valley. It will help you girls realise how we spend our time. It is a far cry from the settled areas where we worked in the old country."

He didn't try to explain it. She had already exclaimed over the many scars and still current wounds that dotted his body, evidence of rigours the men faced in hacking their ways through the mazes of 'The Grose.'

~ * ~

When Charles was six weeks returned to his quest, leaving Martha to her teaching routine, she was daily becoming more convinced of again being pregnant.

"Come autumn, I reckon, Annie."

"Me too, Martha."

They laughed. In both Yorkshire and Scotland they had lived through pregnancies together, coinciding with their men having been home on leave. Here it was happening for the fourth time. But on this occasion they were able to share some knowledge of what their men were going through.

Martha gave Annie snippets from the tracts Charles had left with her.

"Twenty years ago, Annie, when explorers made their first studies of the Grose Valley, the surveyor general's diary was published, and these are extracts…"

To perfect the map of the colony it was considered necessary that as many of the ravines as possible should be traced in order to lay the natural boundaries of counties and parishes. But however easy it may be to give instructions to the surveyor to follow these gullies down, the performance thereof I know by my own experience, as having my full share in that sort of duty, was attended with much difficulty, hardship and privation.

Govett gave up after months of searching in deplorable conditions and adopted the alternative expedient of tracing the tops of ridges and avoiding valley depths.

When a few years later the renowned explorer Paul Strzelecki made his attempt, he noted: "I am likely the first white man other than Govett to ever penetrate that part. Between these ranges lie yawning chasms, deep and winding gorges and frightful precipices. Narrow, gloomy and profound, these stupendous rents in the bosom of the earth are enclosed between gigantic walls of a sandstone rock sometimes receding from, sometimes frightfully overhanging the dark bed of ravines and its black silent eddies or its flowing torrents of water. Everywhere the descent into the deep recess is full of danger and the issue almost impenetrable.

"We became so bewildered in the endless labyrinth of almost subterranean gullies that I was unable to bring my men to safety until after weeks of incessant fatigue, danger and starvation."

For the first time, Martha and Annie came to realise how their men were in considerable danger.

"If any of them gets lost, Martha," Annie summarised, "they might never be found."

Sixteen

Many months later

Captain Martindale of the RE, appointed when Hawkins returned to England, submitted his third report on progress "Up the Grose."

The survey of the Grose has proved a work of even greater labour than was anticipated. Immediately after Parliament sanctioned last session the expenditure of £1,500 especially for this service, I gave instructions that as many men as could possibly work with efficiency should be employed upon it. Since that time, it has been carried forward from both ends of the valley at once, one party being supplied with food and necessaries from the Richmond (Eastern) end, and the other from the Bathurst (Western) end. The two parties are now within about eight miles of meeting; but the progress is unavoidably slow, where almost every inch of the track has to be cut and formed out of the rock.

Charles and his friends were given a copy of the report, so all would understand when told the captain was under great pressure to have the job completed.

"Those eight miles are as the crow flies," opined Walter.

"And we all know, mates, we aren't bloody crows..." This was from Arthur.

"As many leads end at the base of another wall as do others at the top of a bloody waterfall," proffered Charles.

The four friends sat over mugs of tea waiting for the fire to finish cooking dinner. Lamb steaks were a treat after the scanty meals served up every night back in Britain.

The consensus was reached that, irrespective of the unknowns, the finding of the answer was in their hands.

"We can only keep probing every tangent until we find one that ends not at a wall or a precipice, but in sighting a track cut by our mates coming from the west..."

"...Or them finding a track we've blazed."

Next day they were back on the search. The seven in their unit were now split to conserve time into two smaller teams, one of three and one of four, each to work its way along different ravines. Charles, Walter, and Thomas comprised one team, Arthur, unfortunately, appointed to the other.

"But that's the luck of the draw, mate," Charles told him. "Hopefully one of us gets to meet the team arriving from the west."

Charles was appointed team leader, and on the toss of a coin as to which took which prong of the fork, all set off carrying nothing more than a day's food ration each, red flags, a compass, and machetes. Fresh water was available in abundance everywhere. The red flags were simply strips of linen to tie to undergrowth when beating paths not designated by a creek-bed.

Charles tossed another coin to see who would be third man in the queue, attaching the red flags. Walter won the role. Charles and Tom would take turn being the man in front, he with the greatest amount of slashing and clearing to do.

"It's every man for himself when it comes to avoiding leeches," Charles told them. "But be vigilant. We don't want any man coming down sick."

"When leaving a creek bed," Tom said to Walter, "be sure to tie a flag. Where there is none, any man following will simply continue up-stream."

Charles smiled. "It might also be helpful, Walter my boy, to tie a flag where we meet a stream. Otherwise we'll be the ones who continue down-stream when on our way back."

All chuckled as Tom slapped a palm to his forehead.

Travel without bedding or cooking gear was for the purpose of maximising the amount of ground covered in the day.

"If we meet another dead-end in the course of the first four hours, we'll return to base and equip ourselves with camping gear for our second day. That way, with the track already made, we stash our goods at that spot—and so on. We simply leave hours of daylight enough each day to get back to where we camped. Even with the backtracking, we'll cover more territory than trying to cart full gear along as many as three or four dead-end tracks in any day."

The odds seemed to be that, with only eight direct miles to cover, two or three days in the conditions should prove ample to establish the likelihood of a breakthrough.

Late morning when Charles called a halt for their first 'smoko,' allowed under regulations every two hours, they discussed the fact that, in all the months they'd been searching, they'd seen so few natives in the valley. All knew Aborigines forayed in limited numbers more in valleys than on crests, for crests offered less water and hence less feed, either green or 'on the hoof'...

"...but they've never proved war-like," had been the consensus.

Yet few had been sighted in the Grose Valley.

"Not enough food?"

It was known the blacks could find food anywhere, yet it seemed they liked a variety. In The Grose there were parts where little daylight penetrated the canopy of trees, so ground creatures, with the exception of snakes, were rare, as was much of the vegetation that blacks habitually ate.

"And they don't eat snakes. Evil spirits lurk in snakes, they reckon."

"And roos or wallabies live only in grasslands."

So whilst not concerned about danger from 'black-fellas,' Charles kept careful eyes on his compass, ensuring that the watercourse, while meandering in twists and turns, kept generally flowing from a westerly direction. Yet when with what he reckoned were about three hours of daylight left, that they should turn and retrace their steps to collect bedding, a tent, and food for two more days, they came up against a quandary—one to make Charles feel guilty.

I've paid too little bloody attention to how frequently Walt's been placing his flags.

Where they'd been heavily slashing, the way back was clearly identifiable, yet where undergrowth was not so dense, signs illustrating direction to the next flag were either vague or non-existent.

Yet I shouldn't be blaming Walt. I should be blaming the bloody leader!

He called a halt. "In one sense I feel we shouldn't separate. But when the next flag could be right, left, or straight ahead, we've got to bloody find it. And before it's dark."

They had whistles, standard equipment for every man in such a field.

"By now, mates, we're beyond the hearing of anyone but each other. We've no bedding, no warm clothes for the night chill that we know can here be mean... I've some bread and sausage left. What about you guys?"

Walt had sausage and cheese, Tom only bread.

"Let's be on the safe side and each tell our stomach that it's already had dinner. I'm not panicking, but let's be on the safe side in case dark falls before we find the track. We know it's never far to water and maybe, if we find any creek before dark, it mightn't be far downstream before finding a flag. Right now we should go in different directions looking for one. Anyone with any other thought?"

None were experienced bushmen.

"Abos would find food here," the guilt-ridden Walt proffered. "But they know what to look for."

"Bugs and crawlies that live under tree-bark?" Tom asked. "We're not Abos, mate."

"We might have to start thinking like them, Tom," Charles answered with a grin.

Yet he felt confident their present predicament wasn't serious.

"We'll go off in different directions, look for anything recognised from our outward journey. Blow a whistle blast once every minute so we can tell how far we are from anybody else. Last thing we can afford is for anyone to get lost. If anyone hasn't heard a whistle in sixty seconds, he must turn and retrace his steps, blowing his whistle in triple-blasts. The others will respond until all three are together again. Whoever finds a flag, blow six blasts, and the others make for that direction. Okay?"

All agreed, and they split up.

~ * ~

Martha was at the lumbering stage.

"A month yet, Annie, according to my diary, yet he's giving every indication that he's going to announce his arrival any minute."

As part of her writing practise, Martha had begun keeping a diary and had noted, way back in August, that she might have conceived again.

"But just look at my writing then, Annie, it was all over the place."

She turned pages quickly before again turning the book around for Annie to see. "But look here, only four months later—see how it's already starting to look more regular? You'll find the same, for you're making good progress now."

She was proud to be teaching Annie. In fact every Sunday after church, several of the wives came to her cottage with their slates, to work together.

"I've found," she had said to Charles when he was home only a month ago, "that showing them how you taught me has strengthened my faith in what I'm doing. And their interest ensures I don't lag. Every week I have to plan the next week's lesson."

Fred and Will, seven and five, sat in on the Sunday lessons. Annie, just two, was excused lessons. During the week, Martha took time out from overseeing laundry, housework, and cooking chores to sit with the boys, sorting through the lessons in Charles' old reader. On the housekeeping front, other wives helped women in advanced months of gestation with housework on a time-share basis. A few pennies changed hands, yet the emphasis remained on mutual help.

However, their conversation was interrupted when Arthur rode up.

"This is unexpected," Annie remarked, peering through the sitting room curtain to watch him dismount, "he's supposed to be Up the Grose."

And he was agitated.

"I've just come in from the field," he told them. He had only a quick nod by way of greeting for his wife, to immediately sit down beside Martha.

He held her hand.

"There's no need for worry, Martha, for we don't consider it too serious, but Charles and Walt and Thomas have gone missing."

Martha started, jerked her shoulders back as if little Walter had given her belly walls a kick from within. She and Charles had already agreed that if the new babe was a son, he would be called Walter Thomas, and if a girl, then Mary after Charles' mother. But Martha had all along felt sure her new babe was building up to be a Walter. He kicked like a footballer.

Arthur's news was startling.

"We were broken into small parties, and those three was in one, I was in the other. And Wednesday evening, they didn't return to base-camp..."

Martha interrupted, squeezing tightly on his hand. "Wednesday? But this is Friday. Where—"

Arthur held up a palm.

"Mid-morning yesterday, Walt and Thomas arrived back. The three had separated, gone off to search in different directions. They'd kept in touch with whistles, but just when they were expecting Charles to whistle the signal to retrace their steps, for he was team leader, they never got a signal. They blew their own whistles as loud as they could, but Charles didn't reply. They decided to return to report it rather than one go searching, for then we could have ended up with two lost men." He paused for breath.

"What then? Tell me quickly!"

Annie, as lumbering as Martha, struggled up to bring her a lemonade.

"I went with a party of six. By midday we reached the point where those three had the day before separated. We broke into pairs and went off in the three directions, keeping in touch with whistles, but none received an answer. Everybody knows that if lost we are to whistle SOS in Morse code, but we never heard such a signal. I asked to be the one to get quickly back here so a proper search can be mounted. I rode through the night, and right now, Martha, a twenty-strong party with camping equipment and flares for even night searching is packing up to leave. I'm going back with them."

Martha waved away the lemonade.

"Twenty? Twenty men cannot search the entire Grose Valley. What if he's fallen over a cliff and can't answer whistles? How are only twenty men going to search under every bush for Charles when he might be lying anywhere, unconscious or injured? How are—"

She broke off her own tirade to be struggling up out of her chair.

"Where is Captain Martindale? Is he at headquarters?"

"He is leaving with the search party. They may already have left. I am to catch them up after reporting to you."

"Then who is at headquarters? Who is in charge now? I want…"

Arthur held her steady, for he was sure she would topple.

"Martha, everything is in hand. Too many people only adds the danger of more men getting lost."

Martha knew better. "Come, Annie. We'll take your gig."

Annie had parked it where her piebald was in shade. She'd left it contemplating in a nosebag.

Hmph! How can there be too many searching when it's my Charles out there?

"But what can you do, Martha?"

"Round up other wives who will follow me to headquarters. I'll get more action there."

Arthur could see she wasn't to be dissuaded.

"In Captain Martindale's absence, who's in command?"

"I don't know. When I left, they were still establishing who was going."

"Hmph!" she muttered again and turned to Annie, who was putting on her hat.

"Don't worry about hats, Annie. We'll be driving too fast for hats. You drop me in George Street at the market. I'll organise women there to get home and have their men chase after the captain on the western road. You come back here and get every RE wife packing hampers of food and blankets. Then do the rounds picking them up and take them to the search site. Arthur, can you help her do that?"

"No, Martha. I'm leaving for the search site. I'm under orders. I'm trained in field-work and will be more use there. Charles is my best mate, remember? I want to be the one to find him."

She nodded. "Well, what you waiting for?"

He smiled as he smartly saluted, then ran for his horse.

She heard him muttering as he went, and she smiled inside.

"Annie, dear," she said as if suddenly relaxed, "I've got bread in the oven that will be done enough, a stew already cooling by the back door, and the best part of a whole cheese hanging in the meat-safe. Put them in your gig now. Be careful of the stew, it's still hot."

She looked about.

"Now where did I put my *pince-nez*?"

Seventeen

And his entire neck and face were puffed and itchy from bites. And his body was tired. Worst drawback was that his compass was acting up. Sometimes it gave a clear reading, yet even when only a few yards further, it would begin dancing in wild gyrations. His scientific knowledge of minerals wasn't great, yet he recalled something from early RE training that if iron were present, even well below the earth surface, it could disorientate a compass...

...So maybe it's that, but how's a man to know that either? All I can be sure of is that, for most of each day, I've no certainty about which direction I'm heading. And neither can I get a view of anything from anywhere—unless the top of this waterfall I'm heading for can provide one.

He took a little solace, however, in the fact that so far he had not been confronted with finding himself on a pathway he'd already slashed. Or anybody had slashed.

Then I'd know I've been walking in a circle.

And if I were to follow the stream below the fall, either left or right, it would only take me to places where I'd be as lost as now! So what can a man achieve?

And his belly hungered. The small piece of bread he'd had, he'd found on his first night alone to have become saturated despite rolled up in a canvas bag. He'd eaten it nevertheless, along with a third of his sausage. Yesterday he'd denied himself breakfast. Two-thirds of a single sausage was all he had to last him until found. So he denied himself lunch. Fortunately there was water aplenty. Every leaf around was saturated with it. His handkerchief he used as a sponge on the leaves, and every time he felt a pang of hunger, he apologized to his stomach for offering it only the water he could suck from the kerchief.

He allowed himself a smile when remembering last night's 'supper.'

Supper? Hah! A third of a sausage is all I gave my poor stomach during an entire twenty-four hours!

He almost smiled again as his mind flew to his waking thought this morning, that today was Friday, the day Catholics forsake meat.

Thank the Lord I'm not Catholic. It least I'll be able to eat the last of my sausage come supper. Will God then take pity on me? That I'll hear a whistle-blast during the night? Or come morning?

He slapped a hand against the pocket of his dungarees where he'd put the whistle. Hanging on a lanyard around his neck, it had kept waking him if he rolled over on the bare rock. He'd moved it to a pocket.

Yes, it is safely there.

He thought too, on Martha. She would likely not yet know he was missing. Surely his mates would spend a day searching for him before heading back to base to report it. Then it would take time for the news to get back home. He knew too, that she would give each of his boys and little Annie extra hugs, despite they wouldn't realise the danger of being lost in bush such as this.

And my new one? Could Martha have had our new babe yet? It's about now she reckoned it should come.

His mind kept racing around many things.

How I got lost remains beyond me. We were answering each other's whistle-blasts when suddenly mine was the only one. There was not even the trace of one so distant that I'd realise either me or Walt or Tom had strayed too far. There was just a nothing. I tried the loudest blasts I could make, to then strain my ears, but could hear nowt but birds—whip-birds in particular with their shrill cry so like a whistle—that it was the most teasing sound a lost man could ever hear. And I tried Coo-ees until my throat hurt. Yet nothing!

And it's impossible to walk a straight line in this forest. And with my compass acting up... And the hunger!

Aborigines, he knew, would find a wide choice of life-saving sustenance in such dense forest...

But they know what won't poison them!

He'd heard of so many stories about white men lost in the bush eating bark or leaves from this or that tree and suffering agonising illness, sometimes to the point of death.

At least while a man can stay on his feet and keep mobile, there's a chance...

His mind harked back to the many weeks on the *Conway*, the hours he, Arthur, Walt, and Thomas spent trailing lines from the poop, the magnificent fish they'd caught for their families' suppers. One side of his brain kept hinting that he wasn't helping himself by thinking on the luxuries of food, yet he rather listened to the other side—it kept telling him that the thought of feeding it delectable tastes might satisfy his belly's hunger at least for a few moments.

But I can't fool the bastard indefinitely!

Come dusk, despondency returned. He looked at his tiny piece of sausage for a long time before returning it to its canvas bag and sliding it back into his pocket.

"You can have more bloody water, if you want," he told his stomach out loud. "But that's all until sometime tomorrow!"

~ * ~

Martha had more midwives in attendance than likely ever witnessed at a Parramatta birth.

Having at HQ harangued every Royal Engineer with even a skerrick of gold braid on his uniform, rallied women shopping at the market, and challenged shopkeepers to close their stalls and make for the head of The Grose, she was suddenly stricken with the realisation that Walter Thomas was insisting on being born.

It's too soon yet, Walter, you are not yet due!

But he persisted.

Walter was born, bawling but hale, no more than an hour later.

Some good soul at the market had just finished unloading his trap. And several of the ladies shopping, as well as those she had been haranguing, made up a bed in the dray, to get her home.

"I can hear him crying," she said after the event, "which means he is all right. And I feel all right. But it's my husband who needs help. Please go now—help look for him."

The shopkeeper who had driven her home, at the market as dawn broke, entreated other shopkeepers arriving to open up, to instead go with him up The Grose. All townspeople knew its reputation. For many years, excursions had based themselves in the town only to be beaten at every attempt made to 'tame' it.

So Martha's entreaties had found some two score, in all, to go test their bushcraft in searching for her man.

~ * ~

Charles again woke to the sound of whip-birds, their shrill build-up to the whip-crack nearly piercing his eardrums. For the fraction of a second, he again thought it might be a whistle blowing, yet as quickly realised that that hope was no more than wishful thinking. For fully fifteen minutes, he sat studying what he knew only by the name of 'the black-boy grass tree.' His mind recalled from somewhere early after arrival in the land that the stump of the bush, for all the world like a 'head' of grass shooting up from the top of its short trunk, held water. The black man would chew on it when no creek or rock spring could be found. And its pith was edible.

But is this the same? The 'black-boy' grass tree?

He had always reckoned that the tree he now inspected was the one he had studied. Woodcut illustrations, however, could never show much detail, and his mind was now only seeing it from vague memory anyway.

But it could be!

He was, by now, desperate enough to try. If it were the right one, it wouldn't poison him. And it would be sustenance in his own trunk. He had to take the chance.

He hacked at it with his machete.

To take some into my belly is my only hope. I simply must put something inside me. And I know of nowt other.

His mind painted lavish images of sausages and eggs while his nostrils twitched at smells of sizzling bacon. And was the water the pith yielded tasting on his tongue like the strong tea Martha always made?

He suddenly realised he was crying.

Dear God! Me of all people?

He swallowed the pith. Not too much. He was disciplined enough not to get carried away with the wonderful sensation of his throat swallowing anything, let alone something solid enough that it would at least fill a tiny hole in his belly.

If for the next thirty minutes I feel no discomfort, no pains in the gut, then I'll eat more. I've certainly the time to spare.

He had decided it was more than purposeless trying to cover more ground when he didn't know whether it was getting him nearer or further from help. And while he waited for gut pains to begin racking him, he stared about...

...to become even more tentative...

Is it my eyes, or is it that the rocks hereabout are no longer grey or tinged with red, but black?

He rubbed at his eyes, yet it made no difference. The rocks hadn't changed.

He pulled out his compass, and it was going berserk. The needle spun like an erratic top, first this way and then that... Never before had he seen such a phenomenon as not only the rock around him but all the stones that lay about looked so strange. He picked one up and rubbed it with a fingertip... Then with a finger-nail... "It's bloody coal!" he shouted aloud.

Coal simply lying in great lumps on the earth's surface? Entire shelfs of it?

He sat, then, not even realising that his belly didn't ache so much.

In Europe, he was aware, there was always fear that such an essential commodity to life as coal might one day die out. Discovering new deposits occasioned elation.

And here's this wasteland of The Grose with coal evident even right on the bloody surface! A man doesn't even have to bloody dig for it! It's a momentous bloody discovery! Here's the very fuel for driving our trains through this valley, just waiting for us to find the bloody path!

He felt seven feet tall.

But still bloody lost!

So he moved on. He again pulled out his notepad and drew, best he could, where this coal deposit lay in respect of direction of the sun, for he could give it no other designation. Then he chopped off more of the black-boy pith to take with him, chewing and swallowing no more than enough to put some bulk into his belly. And after an hour of struggling through the black dirt, he came to a stream.

And another miracle flashed by his brain.

He quickly looked to the sky to see where the sun was.

"West!" he yelled at the top of his voice.

"It's flowing west!"

It was the biggest and fastest-flowing stream he had seen in his four days of searching. But he tried not to get too excited.

In these valleys, direction of streams twists backwards and forwards. That's proved itself time out of number. I wonder if, a mile hence, as the valley turns, this stream still flows west?

The significance of the discovery, he fully realised, if it were so, was momentous.

He fell prostrate by the stream's edge, his entire face submerged as he gulped copious quantities of the crystal water, savouring every sense of the bulk sliding down his throat.

If the black-fella food is poisoning me, at least this will dilute it.

He rose and hurried on, following the river's path.

And at mid-afternoon, still following it, he knew it still flowed westward.

But what was that other sound he heard?

Is fate playing tricks on my muddled mind, or is it a whistle?

Or more whip-birds?

Is it merely hope in my heart being as unkind as to now disorientate my hearing too?

He fumbled for his whistle, impatient.

Oh, how many times have I imagined the thrill of having to do this?

Do I have strength in my lungs to blow hard enough?

Yet desperation gave him strength enough...

Yes, again—a whistle blast.

He blew not a long blast of joy, but the regulation three short, three long, and three short. Then waited. Every second seemed an hour.

Then it came—several short blasts in quick succession—the regulation response to an SOS.

I am found!

Eighteen

Two years later

Charles and Martha were celebrities.

Martha's vehement appeals that rallied the town to her husband's plight having brought on the early arrival of her baby had sparked the fire of not only the Parramatta public, but the entire colony.

The *Sydney Gazette* took up her cause, and overnight there was public clamour for volunteers to join the search. The army threw its resources into the fray, as many troops endeavouring to ensure that searchers didn't get lost as there were those looking for Charles. Politicians saw value in being to the fore, and every bored thrill-seeker in the community clamoured to be amongst those jostling for space aboard vans emblazoned with company logos—every company keen to make capital of the opportunity by transporting people to the search.

The major problem for search organisers at both the eastern and western camps became not details of mounting the most professional search, but controlling the throngs of do-gooders who persisted in getting in the way. Charles was in fact found not by searchers, but by RE sappers seeking the path from the western approach. He had been quickly recuperated that he could be re-united with Martha, and to meet his new son.

And the fact he was able, once recuperated, to direct the authorities to the substantial coal deposits covered him with added glory. Up to that point, the only coal deposits had been the Hunter Valley to Sydney's north, coal requiring tedious transport by sea.

Whilst no gradients had been taken along the route Charles had chanced on, for he was able to report that he had had to scramble up and down many ridges—"In fact some almost vertical, even if not more than two or three hundred feet high"—at least a path worth further investigation had been found.

"A task easier said than done, if you want my opinion, Mother. We have to find the path I took first, and that in itself is not going to be easy. All we yet have is a 'bridle-path'—one for riders, not even for wagons, let alone locomotives."

And when invited by the gleeful westerners in the isolated town of Bathurst as guest speaker on his adventure in finding a path, he had the dubious job of telling them it was still too early for putting a date to a rail-service into their town.

His unit, part of the Sixth Company Royal Engineers, continued work in The Grose until having to report that all efforts had been to no avail.

The path so accidentally discovered by Charles was officially declared 'The Grose Valley Bridle Path,' by which it would be known for generations to come.

~ * ~

"All that for nothing, Mother."

They were on the way to an RE picnic in the vast Parramatta Park. Martha walked with a parasol in one hand and a blanket clutched under her other arm. Frederick and William at ten and eight were old enough to tote hampers. Five-year-old Annie struggled with a large rubber beach ball, and Charles was stooped, holding the hand of the two-and-a-half-year-old Walter.

Arthur and his Annie followed with their littlies, with Charles' other mates and their families behind in turn.

"But what is this switchback thing you're talking about, Charles? You have already said a line over the top is now considered possible, albeit with two engines?"

"Over the top has always been a probability, despite expensive because of tunnels. All that is now agreed, and monies approved. Getting down the western slope is now the difficulty. Other units are surveying the route while we've been called in to assess a switchback. Many say it can't be done, but I don't agree. Yet it is going to take a lot of work to properly assess it."

"As long as assessing The Grose?"

He chuckled.

"No. It can be done. It's a matter of where and how. All the slopes are steep. We must establish which is the easiest to carve into terraces, assess ratios of level-lengths and grades—and how steep the fall— how many miles of each level to the next. Ideally, Mother, it should be three long levels of several miles each. However, the more scarps and creases in the mountainside, the shorter each level can only be. The extent of excavation and reinforcing of edges needed is another limiting factor. There may have to be bridges within the switchback. So there's considerable 'geometry' to be applied before the question is answered. But the Conway Seven has enough smart-bastards to come up with something."

He chuckled again.

"Didn't the captain send for us in particular when selecting who should do what?"

~ * ~

In 1861, the New South Wales government made two significant decisions on its Western Line. It granted £250,000 for its extension to Bathurst and, with escalation of the railway system also in the north of the colony, decided to mount its own Survey Department.

The first was to illustrate goodwill to western settlers who were highly disgruntled at so much time and money being spent in what had ended up a fruitless search. Now the objective was to illustrate clear intent that the line was indeed moving towards Bathurst. The second meant giving the Department of Railways its own control over surveys. It disbanded the Royal Engineers and offered its proven personnel contracts to work directly for the government. The Conway

Seven accepted, to a man, both discharge from one and a contract from the other.

They were no longer Army, but rather contracted artificers to the government.

So now private citizens with no 'found' accommodation and keep for families, but with a monthly cheque in hand, each for an amount greater than Charles could ever have envisaged earning in England, they en-masse moved west of Parramatta. Blacktown was already a station on the line now extending to the foot of the range. There they moved into rented cottages.

Martha wrote a letter home to advise her change of address, requesting that had her mother already despatched a letter during the last three months, would she re-tell any significant news.

In case that letter, because of the move, doesn't reach me, she explained.

Her mother had been excited when first receiving a letter from the 'illiterate' daughter who left home five years prior, and their correspondence had become regular. It had certainly helped Martha feel less distanced.

Being many months from ever knowing if parents or siblings remained hale, ill, or even alive created a sad sense of loneliness for most immigrants, especially those illiterate. The void in thoughts and memories were, for many, difficult to cope with. Martha's loneliness and stress in such instance, once she could write her own messages and questions, albeit stumblingly for quite a time, was remarkably alleviated. She again felt an integral part of her family. Her ma was into her seventies and her pa getting close. Each, however, remained 'reasonably' hale.

Charles' 'bivouac' was now Lithgow, a hamlet at the western foot of the range, his unit the 'designers' of what was to ever be known as the Lithgow Zig Zag line. It was a steeper drop with longer 'levels' than any among them had ever had to 'tame.'

"Maybe, at more than seven hundred feet, it is the steepest scarp ever a three-level-switchback was designed for," he opined. Yet such challenge only further heightened their determination to best the mathematics required. Every inch of the scarp must be graded, excavated, bridged, reinforced or otherwise manipulated.

"But certainly, Mother," Charles announced when home on weekend leave, "the site offers the best views any surveyor ever clapped eyes on. It is magnificent country, with far below and stretching as far as the eye can see, even with a telescope, endless acres of wheat and sheep pasture."

Nineteen

Ed and Maggie Bourn had set up home in the salubrious Newcastle suburb of Hamilton.

Whilst still a somewhat raw township, Newcastle was the largest rural town in New South Wales. They built an eminently comfortable home on the corner of Lindsay and Beaumont Streets, providing ample room for their fast-increasing family of daughters—now five including Hope, born as their steamer approached the Cape of Good Hope—a nanny, a cook, and a housemaid. A man came in two days a week to keep the extensive gardens trim; gardens to continue an absolute joy to Maggie because back in both Shoreditch and Battersea she had had only concrete-porch approaches to her home.

It was from Newcastle that a rail-line was being built to the far north via the western plains. A line north along the Pacific coast was impossible because of the several large rivers that flowed from the Great Dividing Range. Four such rivers were too wide and too deep to be bridged. Ferries were used to transport people and wagons across. The carriages Ed had brought were already carrying passengers and freight west along the Hunter River Valley to Maitland, beyond which stretched wheat fields and sheep and cattle grazing grasslands further than eyes could see. At a later stage, a line south from Maitland would connect Newcastle to Sydney, yet for the nonce all transport for that connection must be by sea. Rugged mountains and the wide Hawkesbury River prevented vehicular traffic of any description.

The Great Dividing Range spread from the tip of Cape York in Australia's as yet unexplored north to the extremity of the southernmost settlements in its south. It formed a barrier seldom more than sixty miles west of the Pacific coast where towns were being sited wherever convenient shipping access was available. The great benefit of the range was its abundance of large rivers irrigating land along the entire coastal strip.

The benefit of the railroad was that it could move people and freight to Newcastle, because in these early days there were not yet traversable tracks, other than the Hunter Valley, across the range.

"Far better, and far more economical," it was explained to Ed by local politicians, "that a single railway west of the mountains can convey supplies to the interior and return with produce for the port. Newcastle's excellent port facilities, still being extended, provide services not only to and from Sydney, but to the coastal north."

"And the rail link to Sydney?"

"Good heavens, man—the rail-line west from Sydney is proof of how costly is getting a line across mountains. A quarter-million pounds has just been allocated to putting Sydney's line over the top and through to Bathurst. Getting it down the western scarp is requiring a zig zag that is the most adventurous in the world."

"Tell me about it. I look forward to seeing it."

"It's under construction, old chap, but will take several years yet. To every railway man in the colony, the zig zag is providing considerable excitement."

Ed Bourn pledged that at the first opportunity he would indeed go see the world's most adventurous switchback under construction.

~ * ~

The news of a government-sponsored exploration party departing the hamlet of Mildura on the Murray River in the south, in endeavour to traverse the continent to its northern shore, passed by New South Wales residents with scarcely an interest. Most seemed to remark only on the fact that the explorers were outspokenly so pessimistic about what they were likely to find, that they took camels both to ride and as beasts of burden for supplies, rather than horses.

"Their goal is to discover if there is an inland sea that the 'sometimes' rivers plying westward from the range can be flowing into," Charles cracked to nine-year-old Frederick.

"Maybe they'll get lost like you in The Grose, Pa."

Charles smiled. "They won't get anywhere near The Grose, boy, unless they're even more lost than I was. They will be so far west of the range where many suggest there could be desert. Go get your atlas."

He had given Frederick the first atlas published by the government printer. Some of the maps used for it were drafted from those the RE had had a hand in creating. He showed the lad where Mildura stood, the village the Burke and Wills expedition was starting from. It was on the Big Murray River that divided New South Wales from the new colony of Victoria, and he pencilled in a dotted line on the huge blank of the atlas page showing the little that was known west of the Divide.

"This is further west from the Pacific Ocean than any explorer has yet ventured, lad. I at least had water when I was lost, but there is likely desert where these fellows are going. They're deliberately setting off realising they will likely find sand but no water, not even vegetation for wild animals to feed off. Nor even to feed themselves."

"And what about natives? Are they likely to be attacked by Aborigines?"

"Not if there's no water there. And if what I have been told is correct, the blacks will give any party with horses, let alone camels, a wide berth. Aborigines have never seen anything larger than a kangaroo, and the sight of horses keeps them well away."

The other news that bypassed most as too far away to be even meaningful was that beyond the world's biggest ocean, the North Americans were fighting each other. Cotton-growing states, their plantations worked by black slaves brought from Africa, had seceded from the Union to form a Confederacy.

"Why countries have to resort to civil wars to settle their differences of opinion," he put to young Frederick, "I cannot fathom. There's nothing that can't be achieved if people would talk rationally when there's a dispute."

So they let the matter rest. It was so far beyond Charles' area of interest that wondering further about it was pointless.

He spent longer periods away from home now. The switchback had developed from the drafting to construction stage, and massive earthworks were under way. More than a thousand navvies and Chinese coolies initially imported to work the Bathurst gold mines, were shifting tons of earth and rock daily. Keeping them operative in *this* section while dynamite blasting in *those* was an exacting exercise on its own. During the construction, the bivouac centre was the little town of Lithgow at the western foot of the Great Divide. So when home, Charles found himself in demand, Martha summoning help in the boys' education in arithmetic.

"My reading and writing skills, Charles, have progressed. But you know me with numbers. I've no training in them and cannot help the boys. However, both find the challenge of reading and writing a magnet when it comes to one-upmanship over their mates. Frederick in particular feels frustrated that I cannot help with numbers. I can add and subtract all right, but multiplying and dividing utterly defeats me. "

"Why do you say 'Frederick in particular?'"

"William doesn't care for numbers. While Frederick will listen and work things out on his slate, William draws doodles. Do you think him too young?"

"No, but everybody is different when it comes to what interests them in learning, or so tutors told me back home. We were taught to concentrate only on what we had a special interest in. 'Nobody can be a master of everything,' they would say. It makes me happy, girl, that you are teaching the boys as well as yourself. Yes, I'll sit with them on numbers. I'll help Frederick on multiplication and division, and I'll try to win William's interest."

And when all personnel working on the switchback were given a week to spend Christmas with their families, including the Chinese who weren't even Christian but who had to be given a break at some time, Charles presented Martha with her first novel.

"Picked it up from a travelling salesman in Lithgow, girl. Fresh in from England, it is. 'Controversial,' he called it. It's causing a furore back home. The fellow who wrote it reckons man is descended from monkeys. You and me too, girl. I've had time to read bits of it, and he seems to know what he's talking about. He even gives reasons where the Bible is wrong in claiming God made everything in six days. He reckons it's taken a million years."

Martha couldn't bring herself to agree with anybody who said the Bible was wrong.

Surely every other Christian in the world can't be wrong.

But she resolved to try and read it anyway, when not so pressed by important things.

~ * ~

Ed Bourn was a busy man and well fulfilling his role as a director of Wright Brothers.

He had established in Newcastle a company to manufacture railway carriages. He began with second- and third-class carriages because they required less sophisticated appointments than first class. He would continue importing those, although submitted with his order were his personal recommendations as to design. Initially, most of his supplies needed to be manufactured in Sydney; however, he had been gradually introducing additional equipment and training local skills for his own factory. He was indeed proving an astute manager. His overall knowledge of the railway industry, if it could be called such, for it was indeed fast becoming one of the colony's major manufacturing bases as well as provider of employment, was much in demand by government.

He found he was needing to take two or three trips every year to Sydney. It was only a day's journey by steamer, yet with the time he spent in meetings and arguments over what he considered trivial matters and then the time waiting for copies of minutes to be made so he could assemble the crucial points from the waffle, each visit was taking a week to ten days.

"You simply can't imagine the bickering that goes on," he told Maggie once home. "Instead of having only knowledgeable railway men to consider elements involved in designing a railway system for the entire colony, they have politicians, all ignorant of mechanics, influenced only in supporting decisions on branch-lines—satisfying voters in the various constituencies being their only goal. To concede to their demands, we would end up having few mainlines, but dead-end branch-lines everywhere."

"What has to happen to change that?"

"Establish a Railway Authority with its own teeth, to study how best and economically to service all areas, then submit cost estimates for government approval. The present system of having committees for every aspect involved at meetings every three or four months is never going to get anywhere. Do you know what happened here before we arrived, even in deciding what rail gauge to use?"

Maggie laid her crocheting in her lap and looked over her *pince-nez*.

"Now how could I possibly know that, dear?"

Rosa and Jessie, the two older daughters who sat over tapestries, giggled.

Ed smiled. "Giggle you may, my dears. But do you recall, Maggie, when Gladstone was Secretary for War and the Colonies? It was during our latter years at Shoreditch. He recommended that all colonies adopt the British rail gauge of four foot eight and a half inches. South Australia was the first colony here to lay a railway line and dutifully laid its Adelaide to Port Adelaide track accordingly. Here in New South Wales, an Irishman, F. W. Shields, was first engineer, and he wanted six foot one. After a series of disputes with Victoria, which wanted the standard gauge, it was agreed they split the difference at five foot three inches, so Victoria built its Melbourne to Hobson's Bay line at five foot three."

Maggie took off her *pince-nez* to watch him. She smiled. The girls also waited.

"South Australia, still seeking uniformity, built its next line at five foot three inches—and of course had to then buy different bogies for every carriage, as well as special engines for that different gauge. In Sydney, Shields resigned over a pay dispute to be replaced by a Scot named Wallace. Now this is where the farce mushrooms...

"...Wallace would have nowt to do with decisions made by the Irish—even those of a Sassenach were, in his opinion, preferable. So NSW laid four foot eight and a half inches.

"The colony of Queensland's First Engineer was another Irishman, Abraham Fitzgibbon, who decided that three foot six would be more economical, so Queensland established another standard. South Australia looked with envy at the savings Queensland was making, and with one four foot eight and a half inches line and one at five foot three, began laying three foot six and ordering from England, yet a third width of bogies and, again, special engines for that line. South Australia, my dears, now has no inter-connecting lines. Nor can it ever have. Every item of freight being trans-shipped to anywhere else must be unloaded and re-loaded at the Adelaide terminal. It has different line gauges at all its three platforms. What is going to happen when the several colonies link-up with each other's borders is going to be absolutely chaotic."

Maggie stopped smiling and looked bemused.

"Surely you are joking, Ed. I cannot imagine this is true."

"Believe it, my dear. The entire thing is an absolute farce. It is suggested by many that one day in the not too distant future, the colonies on this continent will join into a federation—like the American system. So don't you feel it would only be common sense to all agree on something rather than look forward to the eventual costs of restarting? The meeting in Sydney I have just attended remains pretty much a case of having such ill-conceived ideas debated."

The women all fell to giggling.

"Surely that couldn't happen in England, Dad?" asked Rosa.

"Never. There is only a single governing body for the entire United Kingdom railway system. Gladstone was severely rapped over the knuckles over letting this happen. Nothing is changed. Each colony here has a sovereign right to make its own decisions. It will take a new bill in Parliament there, but who is going to meet the costs of re-laying so much track here? So you can see what I'm up against, trying to manufacture for local railways, whether it be bogies or spare parts or carriages. Every colony is using different width bogies."

"What do you see as the answer?"

"Each sitting down in the hope of three out of four electing to relay all their tracks is an exercise doomed to failure. The horses have bolted and can never be recaptured is the way I see it. But to establish some sensible governing body here in New South Wales, we must institute the body I mentioned—establish a Railway Authority with its own teeth. And that is what I am promoting. At every meeting, I am insisting that that is what we need."

~ * ~

Martha let her fortieth birthday slip by, hoping nobody would notice. And it was not difficult to let it slip by with Charles away for so many months at a time.

But then he is one who attaches little importance to birthdays, particularly his own—and to an extent, even the children's. And mine. It's his wont, it has ever seemed, never to even diarise them.

'Somebody will always remind me, Mother,' he will say, and when I then explain that would invariably be later than having opportunity to prepare a gift, or at least a card, he responds with caustic comments on the senselessness of giving importance to dates in history when something happened. 'Life is a today thing, woman,' he will proclaim. 'Yesterdays should be forgotten unless to remind us of foolish things we have done, lessons to prepare us against repeating them.'

Martha continued purchasing birthday presents for the children and declaring on the card, 'With sincere love from your Pa and Ma.' *Sometimes I don't even bother getting something for me. Not while he's off in the field at any rate. When he's home, I simply give him plenty of notice.*

But he hadn't been home in six months, so there hadn't been opportunity to give him notice anyway.

But he continues to write, so is still thinking of us.

'Work on the switchback is proceeding at a frenetic rate,' Charles had written.

"I have finished reading my book," she told Annie. "And in the main I can now understand at least the gist of what he is telling us. He is obviously a learned man—travelled much of the world studying not only creatures, but people, endeavouring to learn why every next generation arrives into the world with some features different, depending on the environment they live in. Quite engrossing, yet hardly creditable in the overall scheme of things. Yet many scientists believe he can be touching on fact."

"What, that we are descended from monkeys?"

"Well yes, but not like that sounds. It is more complicated. He seems to think life started off with maybe this and maybe that sort of creature and each kept changing over several generations, and people are one of those sorts of extensions. The thing that leans me towards his theory is how all mothering creatures are so protective of their little ones. That's something common to every creature for thousands of years, so there's a bond, isn't there?"

Annie didn't answer. She had only a confused expression on her face.

"Just look at you, for instance," Martha said, hands a-hip. "Your face one big question mark. I just wish you could read the things he says for yourself. I can't put them in his words because I'm not educated like him. But reading what he wrote, I could not turn a page without feeling right down inside that there is a lot of sense in the picture his words have put in my mind. I think he has lots of things in his favour."

"Even about the monkeys?"

"Well maybe not quite that far. But you still have to admit the big apes are pretty much like people. They can walk on two legs.'"

She sat at the table and laid a palm on the book.

She didn't want to agree with all it claimed, yet neither did she want to denigrate. It had moved her. She let her fingers caress the heavy gold embossing on its leather cover.

Mr. Darwin's chosen a subtle green for the colour—quite proper for a book so much about nature. And he's gone to so much trouble with so many woodcut illustrations to describe some of the changes taking place. He couldn't do that if what he's saying isn't true.

And every page with woodcuts had a tipped in sheet of bible paper to stop ink rubbing off from one illustrated page to another.

It's just that everything about the book is so professionally done that it gives credence to what Mr. Darwin says.

Twenty

Several years later

Edward Bourn won a major victory in Sydney. He had advised the government transport minister that he was journeying to inspect the completed switchback and that on arrival back in Sydney, he wished to present a five-year plan for railway development in New South Wales. He nominated the particular personnel he hoped would be present, and added the footnote "...And I guess any few others to whom you feel under some obligation to include."

He smiled as he wrote that. If he read the minister as well as his alter-ego assessed the man, he too would read between the lines and smile.

In only five days he received the most positive of replies.

I shall call a meeting for September 16. That will give you time to set a timetable to visit Lithgow and return to Sydney. I have invited those you named and felt obliged to include three others (who will be out-numbered when it comes to a vote). You know you have my support if your proposal is as worthy as your input to date. Advise the

*date you expect to reach Lithgow so I can arrange for you
to be met and given a personal inspection.*

The Edward Bourn family had, during the interim, increased by another daughter, Maude. Maggie continued apologetic at not presenting Ed with a son to replace the 'little Ed' they buried as a tot, and Father Ed had no option but to accept what arrived.

"Six daughters, however," he told the family, lined up in order of age—Rosa, Jessie, Edie, Eliza, and little Hope—ten years through four, "is a feat in itself to be proud of. In fact I'm beginning to wonder if I might be able to pull strings somewhere in this colony, to introduce the system of suitors paying dowries to the parents of brides. In which case, my dear, I might be calling on you to continue bearing daughters forever more."

She bobbed him a curtsy as all the girls giggled.

And he was indeed impressed with the switchback. Before leaving Mt. Victoria station on the edge of the western scarp, he had asked the guard to alert him when approaching it and had been all agog with anticipation—and had certainly not been disappointed.

Now that second and even third-class carriages had roofs, an improvement in which Ed himself had had significant input, them having been made in Wright Brothers' very factory in Newcastle, first-class carriages were now situated immediately behind the coal-wagon. This meant he could, with all confidence, let down his window enough to take sneaky looks out when on the inside of curves, to see the track ahead.

"Though not that one felt overly confident looking down from the other side," he admitted to the 'guide' appointed to him on arrival. "From the left side when the train was curving to the right, one couldn't help but feel the rails were too close to the shored-up ledge. It seemed like a vertical drop into nothingness—not an experience for the faint-hearted, eh?"

"Yet I assure you, sir," said the guide, who illustrated first-hand knowledge of every facet, "that all is extremely safe. The mix of the fill, gradients of the rail and angles of the scarp have been calculated to assist each other to the most exacting formulae. The surveying engineers were all ex Royal Engineers with years of experience in the old country. The entire project is an excellent example of our art's modern techniques."

"Well thank you, Charles. But forget the 'sir.' This is not the old country. I find the local custom of familiarity with names, unless on formal occasions, a compliment. I am known as Ed. You were with the RE in Britain, then? Whereabouts?"

"Surveying the line Holyhead, the Goole to Hull, then the Glasgow environs. But this little exercise has been the greatest challenge ever."

"What's next for you?"

"Bathurst. My family is in Blacktown. You'd have passed through it just this side of Parramatta. I guess we'll soon be moving to Bathurst. It depends on the territory we must graph between here and there."

"Plans are in hand for lines north, south, and further west from Bathurst. Do you know the district well?"

"No. But I'll be there until the surveys are done, four or five years. Then I'm not sure what the Rail people have in mind. They seem a bloody rabble the way they keep changing their minds on things."

Ed coughed—yet as quickly grinned.

"I know what you mean. But I think the upper echelon is starting to get some better organisation into things. It's not easy in a new land with many unknowns. I hoped you might have some thoughts on the actual routes extending from Bathurst."

"West is a worry. You heard about the Burke and Wills fiasco, I'd reckon. The country out west doesn't look too bright for grazing either sheep or cattle."

The Burke and Wills expedition had not only discovered no inland sea, but land so inhospitable that most died—either by starvation or at the hands of hostile Aborigines.

"Oh, that is too far west. I'm thinking of areas Oxley discovered—along the Lachlan and up the Macquarie. There's development out that way, I hear."

"Oh, my word, Ed. There's great rejoicing from those areas. They're counting the days towards the line reaching Bathurst at least."

Ed smiled again and said no more. However, he invited Charles to dinner at his Lithgow hotel. He not only wanted to say 'thank you,' but to sound him out on his experiences since arriving in the colony.

"It is always an interesting topic when discovering a man who arrived only a matter of months of one's self, yet whose time has been occupied in quite a different facet of railway work."

He came away impressed with the fellow. *One obviously of considerable confidence and ability—and with a sensible grasp on finding his way in a raw community.*

Back in Sydney, Ed found himself among, on this occasion, men ready to concentrate strictly on major goals without being sidetracked by biased detail. He presented what he considered likely areas for inspection as rail services, areas like Mudgee and Dubbo, Cowra and Young. And feeders of the already progressing southern line snaking its way to Melbourne. He was able to report on the line north from Maitland.

The minister was personally impressed enough to call for agreement to carry out inspections on the areas Ed proposed. And received it.

"We are still a long way from even seeing where there might one day be a Crewe-type junction with tendrils joining up major lines," Ed told Maggie.

"And how was the switchback?"

He gaped. "Ah. It's absolutely tremendous, bigger and better than anything we had to build in Britain—ever built in the world, I wouldn't be surprised. Those RE men came up with a top-rate answer to that impasse."

~ * ~

In the same month Lee surrendered what was left of the American Confederacy to the Union, Maggie, in Newcastle, New South Wales, at the age of forty-three, presented her Ed with a seventh daughter they named Emily.

And in Lithgow, a year later, an aghast Martha told Charles that she thought she was pregnant again after seven barren years.

"And I'm forty-five, Charles."

"That means, girl, you'll be having it in February," said the astonished Charles, "in late summer. Summer here in Lithgow, girl, is bloody hot as I discovered last year. Maybe we should think of you travelling east—back to Parramatta—or even Sydney, for the birth."

Charles knew he couldn't leave. With the switchback work finished, they had moved from Blacktown to Lithgow, now 'home' base while the line further west was surveyed. He was a section boss now, and whilst no longer in the army, his was still a 'duty calls' role. It would be leaving his mates in a bind if he took extended leave to move back east with Martha. So he took two weeks 'compassionate leave' when Martha was five months, during most of which, for the first time in a pregnancy, she was ill. Then when the western plains summer was beginning to hit the century, they took the train back east. Martha decided to 'lie in' at Parramatta. Arthur's Annie and other wives would, between them, care for the Richardson littlies.

"In Parramatta I will feel more at home than Sydney, Charles. And I've friends here. And the same doctor and midwife who attended me with Walter. So you can return to Lithgow and your work. I'll be all right alone. We can write each other. When I know the time is getting close, I'll tell you. But I don't want to drag you all that way. Once it's born I'll write, and then you can come. What will we call it if it's a boy, or if it's a girl?"

"Something different, Mother."

She laughed. "That's the first time you've called me Mother in ages. I've liked you calling me 'girl.' 'Mother' was what you called me when we were having regular littlies, so I suppose it is appropriate again now. But what should I call it if you're not here?"

"Martha if a girl and John if a boy. This will hopefully be your last, so I'd like a daughter named after you. If a boy, it's behove on me to call a son John. We already have our 'William' name, and Frederick is our 'Charles.'"

And as he expected, she agreed.

John Henry Richardson was born come February and was to prove, despite her illness while carrying him, sound and healthy.

Charles jumped on a train the very evening he received Martha's letter, to bring his family home—not to Lithgow, but to Bathurst, which had become more-or-less home base for all the survey team.

~ * ~

"Well, this is exciting news, Maggie."

"What is that, dear?"

Ed was reading the *Newcastle Herald*.

"It says here that Sydney has its first telephone installed. It's in the governor's office."

"Well, it's not much use to him. When is the second to be installed?"

He laid down the paper and laughed. "What a cynical response!"

"I couldn't resist it. It simply seemed a worthless exercise installing one. I would have expected the article to inform us who the governor can call. His wife at home, maybe?"

Ed scanned the rest of the article.

"It simply says that people and business houses are clamouring to have the service installed. It will be governed, of course, by where cables can be strung... Ah, here..." He read:

> *The installation of street-poles to carry electric power lines for the lighting of Sydney, to replace gaslight, is already under way. The same poles will carry telephone cables.*

"So like everything else in a growing community, my dear, development of any one innovation is governed by the development of others. It is certainly a milestone in the colony's history."

"Well, talking about the government, what was that official-looking envelope that came yesterday? Anything marked 'Strictly Confidential' is always a tease. I will understand, of course, if you tell me you cannot answer."

He folded his paper and put it down, then gave her a wry smile.

"It is from the Ministry of Transport. I have known about this for a little time, yet decided not to tell you until all was confirmed. You know I have been campaigning for some time for the government to create an administrative body over railways...?"

He waited until she nodded.

"...Well, my appeals have been heard. I was approached to take a leading role. This letter informs that only now pending formal parliamentary approval of an addendum to the act, I have been appointed *Inspector of Rolling Stock* for NSW Government Railways."

"Oh!" Maggie clasped hands to her chin.

She knew 'Inspector' was rail language for overall manager of divisions.

"I wasn't going to tell you until that final step happened. However the appointment is now merely a rubber-stamping. I have to resign my position with Wright Brothers, or 'conflict of interests' can be claimed by the more democratically minded, but my government salary and benefits will far outstrip the loss of that income. So your husband is to become a civil servant, my dear, with considerable teeth in respect of what decisions are made regarding railways."

She put down her crochet and came to put her arms around his shoulders. "My clever man. You know I have ever been proud of my husband. And especially now. Congratulations, my dear."

They kissed.

"Does that mean we must move to Sydney?"

He read concern in her expression.

"Well, not at the moment, anyway. I discussed this with the minister. He is prepared to wait until I gain some measure of running things from here. I shall certainly have to spend considerable time in Sydney. The Everleigh Workshop has become a huge complex since we started building locomotives, and it now comes under my jurisdiction. So maybe two weeks in every month I shall need be there. I will take rooms close to it. They will provide a woman to keep the house and cook for me."

Maggie returned to her crochet and worked quietly for several seconds.

"It would be sad if we had to leave the comforts we have built here. And the girls are happy here. It would be a particular wrench for the older ones. So now, my dear, it seems the time to tell you a little secret, which could touch this same matter. Rosa wants to marry her Bill Manuell. They have next year in mind. I'm not sure when. She asked me not to say anything to you until Bill formally approaches you on it. But your news now does raise the fact that all our older daughters are coming up the age of having beaux. If we had to move now, it could prove difficult in that respect.

"Keeping tabs on now seven daughters is to likely prove difficult enough work for any man," Ed joked. "I take your point, and heartily agree. Yet that problem is for the future. Let us see how things go. I will say nothing to Rosa before Bill approaches me. Does your silence on it indicate your approval?"

"Oh yes. I consider him an excellent young man for her. And she is indeed very much in love with him."

"Then I shall welcome him as a prospective son-in-law."

Twenty-one

The Richardson family was settling into its 'new' house.

It had had several—Whitgift, Glasgow, Hobart, Parramatta, Blacktown, Lithgow and now Bathurst. And they realised that, with Charles' work, home would always be transitory.

It was a 'gold' town, the first town settled west of the range, which meant it carried the 'frontier' designation, expanding as people migrated into the western plains to begin growing wheat or grazing sheep or cattle. Bathurst became the centre for supplies and local government to newly arriving settlers. And when gold was discovered in 1852, the field was so rich that thousands of hopeful Diggers flooded in.

Martha received, not long after moving there, the sad news of her father's passing. Billy and Sarah Billing had moved back to Brixworth after Martha left, invited back by Sarah's brother. It had been her father who took exception to Billy's vagabond lifestyle, yet brother Robert found work for Billy 'back home.'

"Seventy-seven, he was Charles," Martha explained. Correspondence with her mother had become regular since Martha's accession to the educated ranks. "And it makes me happy he could be buried at All Saints by his three little Josephs. That made Ma happier, too."

Charles watched Martha as she sat back having said that, her face a picture of one momentarily transported back to her beloved Brixworth—to All-Saints in particular.

She never complains about me having taken her away from all that, although I know she misses it.

He realised his good fortune in having such a life partner. She had ever simply picked up her possessions and children whenever his work demanded another move. *And I don't really think she's happy here in Bathurst. It's good for her, though, that we still have Arthur and Annie by our sides. Annie's become almost a sister to her despite being left far behind when it comes to understanding things. In that department, Martha has advanced by leaps and bounds.*

There was great frivolity in the town when the first train puffed its way into the 'middle west.' Great arguments had raged as to where to locate the station. Some had wanted it east of the river and others west, so the council refused to do anything about widening or sealing roads until a decision was made. Every street in the town, therefore, after storms, became sticky mud. All that, however, was now behind them. People not only had streets being paved, but a train to connect them, via the switchback, over the Divide to Parramatta and Sydney. And it was now a comfortable journey for those wanting to escape the heat of summer, to travel to Blackheath and Katoomba, the towns atop the Blue Mountains range. It was such a contrast in the weather, up there, that it snowed on occasional winters.

"And the Cobb & Co. doesn't mind losing its livelihood now the stage is not needed here. It simply moves further north or south or west, to service emerging new towns."

~ * ~

Martha waited anxiously as Charles tore open the envelope.

It wasn't easy. He was a tall man, his large hands adorned with the scars of many small wounds, of one apprenticed to carpentry and who had spent a lifetime since working outdoors in all sorts of weather. His thumbs were perforce large and rough from scrabbling in rubble.

It was an envelope printed with the crest of NSW Government Railways and addressed to Charles Richardson Esquire, Surveyor, c/- Stationmaster, Bathurst, NSW. The stationmaster had sent it to Charles at home, by a boy on horseback.

It was not a long letter, but meaty.

Martha's shoulders twitched, and the question on her face had developed almost into a scowl. "Hurry up, Charles. Who is it from?"

Charles slowly rubbed a hand on his chin.

"Do you remember me telling you of the Londoner now living here in Newcastle? The man who came to inspect the switchback? Edward Bourn?"

Martha's scowl dissipated as the questioning look returned. She nodded.

"I gathered he was some sort of bigwig but I didn't know he was about to become the government's bloody Inspector of Rolling Stock. That puts him right up there among the bigwigs."

Martha started twitching again as Charles paused, thinking on that.

"Well, why is he writing to you? Hurry up, Charles!"

"He is coming to Bathurst next month and wants to talk with me about The Great Northern Line. He wants me to reply if I can meet him off the afternoon train twelfth March."

"Well, you can. Can't you?"

"Yes, Mother."

"Does he say he wants you to go live in Newcastle?"

"I've just told you all he says. I will reply that I can meet his train. I suppose he will then want to book into a hotel."

"I'd recommend The Macquarie, Charles. I should think he can afford the best."

"Maybe you'd like to offer him the spare bed on our veranda?"

"Huh."

She considered his joke in poor taste.

"Or you could move Frederick and William to the veranda so he can have their room?"

She didn't answer. *Oh, he can be so exasperating at times!*

I'll bet that right now she's thinking how exasperating I get at times.

Yet I know he can read me like a book. I'll change the subject… "Annie and her Freddie are talking of marrying fourteenth May. Do you see anything wrong with that?"

"I've nothing planned so far ahead."

"She wants to marry at the church. Is that all right with you?"

"Of course. That's still the usual thing, isn't it?"

"Yes, but you never go to church any more."

"Well, I'm away from home so often one gets out of the habit. And so long as the kids stay healthy, why do I need to go to church?"

Martha looked to the ceiling then shook her head.

When he gets into these moods it's best to just walk away.

She walked away.

~ * ~

Charles took Martha's sulky to meet Ed Bourn off the afternoon train. He drove him to the Macquarie Hotel, where Ed booked in for overnight. He would leave on the morning train.

"Do you enjoy a drink, Charles?"

"I do that, thanks, Ed."

"Then let us repair to the guest lounge and chat over what I have here to show you."

He chose a large table to spread out his map of the Hunter Valley and points north.

"The Hunter River is wide, Charles. It can only be bridged a few miles upstream, but the city itself, and pretty well all its suburbs, are spread across this large isthmus between the river to its north and the ocean to its east. It is currently a boom city with a wealth of rich, high-grade coal on its doorstep, seemingly without end. It extends west through the entire valley. The railway currently runs from the wharves due west through the valley to Maitland, where the western plains begin. The city is, after Sydney, the largest deep-water port on the continent's entire east coast. Because of such massive coal deposits, we have what is building to be a bigger steel-works than even Sydney can boast. We also have the biggest railway-carriage factory on the entire continent and already have foundries building bogies and even small locomotives. All in all, we are experiencing a population explosion.

"We already have nine churches and a large theatre. *The Victoria* boasts more than two hundred dress circle seats, more than four hundred stalls, and the pit holds a further five hundred. The population is growing so fast we need the railway to begin servicing the people as well as freight. A suburban grid is needed."

Charles wondered that the man didn't even pause for breath.

"Having witnessed what you achieved on the switchback, I am hopeful I can persuade you to bring your family to Newcastle. I can offer you two guineas a week more than you received surveying the Bathurst route. And when that work is done, there is plenty of challenge on the Northern Line. I plan to have it reaching the Queensland border within five years, and there are the New England Tablelands to conquer."

Wow, this does seem a long-term project. One to take me right up to retirement. But where did he get my bloody salary from? And my address to send me that letter? Obviously from someone with access to my records. So he's gone out of his way to come to me in particular. And we only met once.

"That's sounds generous, Ed. And yes, a man reaches a stage of life when he should be settling down after ever being on the move. A frontier town like Bathurst isn't ideal. Maybe it could be Newcastle."

"That is sound thinking, Charles. It is good to hear a man who's spent an itinerant life talking of settling down. I recommend Newcastle. I had to move my family from London, and fortunately, Newcastle didn't disappoint us too much. And it has grown considerably since. I have seven daughters, Charles, so know the value of having a settled type of life. Newcastle's been lucky for me."

"I've but one daughter along with four sons. She's planning to wed mid-May. I'd not like leaving before that. But how can I get an idea of costs for houses in Newcastle? If my wife likes the look of it, once arrived, I'd buy one to settle down in."

Ted smiled. "Is that a 'yes?'"

"Given some idea of house costs, yes. My eldest son works with me, and I can recommend the quality of his work. Taught him myself, I did. Would there be work for him?"

"Indeed. This is a growing colony, and the impetus seeming to increase each year. I will need to check that out with the appropriate department, and you know what governments are like. At the moment, they seem to be giving me a free hand at things. He would have to be prepared to work for regulation pay. And it is higher there than in rural Bathurst—city prices of lodgings and all that. I shall let you know."

Charles waited while Ed made notes in a pocket-book.

"I shall reply in about a week, Charles. If all is then satisfactory for you, we can arrange the transition for after your daughter's marriage?"

They shook on it, and Charles drove the sulky home, his mind whirling.

How's Mother going to react to this? Walking out on her only daughter straight after the girl's marriage?

<h1 style="text-align:center">Twenty-two</h1>

"Oh, Charles. I've never lived in a city. It seems exciting, yet leaving our Annie here alone? Oh dear."

"The girl is getting married, Mother. She has to leave our house anyway. She has to start making her own life with her husband, same as you did. Same as every girl does. Your ma had to. We'll be writing often, and once we get the feel of the place, we can see how things lie for her Freddie finding work in Newcastle. That's a possibility to keep in mind."

"And you get a better pay-slip there?"

"Two guineas a week. That's more than a hundred pounds a year extra. We'll be able to afford a nice house. Ed said developers are building houses by the dozen now the city's growing so quick. So there'll be many to choose from."

Frederick and William were now twenty-three and twenty-one, Walter and John fifteen and eight. Ed had affirmed there were schools in the city for the younger lads, although Martha wasn't keen on John going to boarding school.

"Maybe they can be day students, Mother. Many schools offer choices these days. But we can sort that out once arrived. It's Annie we've to make plans for. Her Freddie's got his carpenter's ticket, and there's work all over the west with new settlers flooding in. I can give him a kick-start with twenty quid."

And they did.

Annie married her Freddie Jones at the Cathedral Church of All-Saints.

And it somewhat appeased Martha's mind that Bathurst's church had the same name as Brixworth's.

After a three-day honeymoon in the mountain town of Blackheath, chilly and with fogs so thick that coaches couldn't operate at night—"and during the days can only travel at a walk," Annie told them on arriving home, "...and even then, ringing bells because the driver can't see more than a yard past the lead horses' ears,"—it was time for her parents and brothers to leave.

And there were farewell tears aplenty.

Annie and Freddie would stay on in the house Charles had been renting.

"She has that familiarity to hold on to, Ma. She will feel our presence here until she's ready to leave it."

Yet it was Arthur's Annie who seemed the most distressed.

"What shall I do without you, Martha? I realise now how much I've depended on you—ever since Whitgift. And every place we've moved since. I do wish we were going, too."

"When you live without fences, Annie, there is no greener grass elsewhere. You learn to live where and with what you have. Same as our own Annie has to. You must simply climb out of bed every morning ready to get stuck into every new day—make your own life."

I know my new day will dawn in Newcastle. I too am sad at losing a dear friend's company and support, but, as Charles says, changes simply have to be made the best of.

And as if aware of her thoughts, he right then put his arm around her waist.

"Nothing quite so exciting, Mother, as when adventure pummels at one's nerves. There is always excitement when crowds gather like this."

They were at the station, their all having been forwarded on as freight.

He had taken her moment of silence being disappointment at having to leave not only daughter Annie, but her namesake friend.

It's not that I should be trying to bolster her confidence. She has enough. It's just to make her more quickly cut the cord—have the maudlin bits done with.

The engine was loudly hissing as if anxious to be on its way. *As anxious as I am to be getting on with our new life.*

He hated partings. He wanted to get stuck into his new job in the new town—hopefully where he could settle his family down. Even the journey ahead held little appeal. He wanted to be there.

And I should not have to feel apologetic about cutting short all this kissing and cuddling.

So while the boys were queued up to hug their sister, he gazed about at the milling throng. "Do you ever wonder, Mother, how many of those who come to a station to see others off are simply anxious to see them gone?"

She wiped away a tear and shook her head.

"What? Want to see the back of them? Want to make sure they really leave?"

He chuckled. *That's certainly bloody likely when it's a man's mother-in-law leaving! But a man can't say so.*

Instead, he continued on the meat of the subject. "You think that's why Annie and Freddie might be here?"

"No! They are genuinely sorry to see us leave."

"All the more reason, then, to get these farewells over quickly and settle ourselves inside. She has her Freddie now. She has her own new life to settle into."

The door to their first-class compartment was already open, and further down the platform the guard was calling, "All aboard."

Charles helped Martha up the step and into the compartment. But his own anxious egress was thwarted when she paused, blocking his way. She bent down to straighten a stocking seam, to only then take a seat before wiping away another tear. He sat by her and took her hand.

And when final waves were done, the train jerked into what seemed its own painful departure, inching its first yard before settling into its rhythmical clickety-clack.

The boys then, the family having the compartment to itself, settled back by their respective windows.

Martha was first to speak.

"When we arrived in Tasmania, Charles, no one wanted us. They hadn't bothered about telling us about the changes in the programme. Then when we arrived in Sydney, they sent us out to Parramatta that was no more than a struggling village—a nice house, yet a place with no services. And the people all so strange—almost a different race. If we hadn't had the Conway Seven around us, we'd have remained strangers. It was strange enough being away from England. How can we really know what to expect in Newcastle?"

"Colonies are like that. All are their own separate entities and develop their own styles around what happens. In Britain, lifestyles are much the same, even though it's different countries. Everybody is either insular or outgoing, same as everywhere else, but their lifestyles are settled into the routines of centuries. Here all colonies are rivals trying to forget the land started out as a prison. Sometimes I feel the people's attitude to life is so apologetic that no one wants to talk about the past. Everyone seems to live only for a future. There is little that is static. It's everything continually changing that I find so exciting about the place."

"I can see that. I find excitement too, but maybe that's because we've been able to make independent decisions about what we do..."

"Like deciding to come to Australia? And now moving to Newcastle? Yes, it's a land of people making decisions for themselves, not simply following leaders. We came at the beck and call of the RE, to remain so for a long time—but now we're free to make our own decisions."

He was conscious of the older boys, at least, lending ears.

"But someone else made the decision about Newcastle, this Ed fellow?"

"Absolutely. Ed Bourn made the decision to invite us—yet it was our decision to accept. We've nowt to lose by having a look at the place, Mother. That's all I've committed to. It's not the RE, girl—it's still up to us to do something different if we don't like the place. But all the advantages offered are worth a look-see."

Martha watched her Frederick and William exchanging quiet little nods.

Well, they see how Charles is right in all that, of course. They realise there'll be more opportunities for them in a big town. And Ed Bourn did send an authority for us to come first class, even aboard the steamer from Sydney. So all this illustrates his good intentions. And Charles hasn't been proved wrong very often. It's just that he doesn't include me in such big decisions.

"You say 'our decision,' Charles. Yet we never discussed it. You simply accepted the offer."

Charles didn't feel winded. "What alternative did I have? What was in Bathurst as a future? Ours or the boys? Moving to Newcastle is no different from making the decision to leave England, and the only objection you raised then was fear of convicts. We need to find a place to settle down. In ten or maybe fifteen years, I'll be retiring, and I don't want to spend my old age crawling about scarps and gullies surveying railroads. I want you and me to have somewhere comfortable where we can settle back. And in between, somewhere where I can work local instead of 'out in the field.'"

She sat quietly, her mind still racing. *Frederick and William born in England, Annie in the middle of the ocean, Walter and John here. They're growing up with no roots like I had in Brixworth.*

"With all this moving around the world, Charles, do you ever feel sad about leaving your birthplace?"

"Northampton? Hunger and shivering is how I remember my birthplace. I hated it. We were so poor when Pa died I had to quit school at twelve when sent away from home. Yet I was lucky, I now realise. That change in my life turned out to be the best thing that could have happened. I never discovered a real happy home until moving to Brixworth. And meeting you. It's childhood memories that made me swear an oath to myself that I would never pass up the opportunity of ensuring a secure future for my family. And I'm still doing it. Newcastle has many advantages for kids growing up that Bathurst lacks. Newcastle is already destined to be the city to service the entire north of a colony four times the size of the entire United Kingdom. Think on that, girl. And our kids..."

He pointed around to each of the boys, all four now paying attention to what their pa was saying, not loudly, but quietly enough to command attention. "Our children's births? Our first two were in England, yes! Annie was registered here, so that means our local children outnumber the foreigners! But it makes us an international family. So what really is the 'home' that you say Brixworth is to you? I'm happy for you having somewhere to feel envious about, but we aren't there, girl, we're here! You are right in saying that none of our kids have a Brixworth to dwell on, but they've grown up in a world of change. Newcastle, if we can happily settle there, can begin illustrating a settled-down way of life—something Brixworth became a thousand years ago. Our kids have a different understanding about what is 'home and heritage.' My challenge is to make Newcastle somewhere that becomes more of a settled home than only you have any experience of."

He sat back then, waiting, watching all five of his family. The boys were not watching him but seemed waiting on their Ma. And after what seemed a full minute, he laid a reassuring hand on her thigh.

She did no more than nod slowly, then move her hand to cover his.

For several minutes nobody spoke and the boys started to again peer out their windows.

"Just you wait, my dearest," Charles then said so quietly she was conscious of young John shifting his seat closer so he could hear better. "I promise when we reach Newcastle you will make new friends. This Ed, for instance, has seven daughters to help make up for missing Annie. I'll be thinking of all of you—you, girl, and every one of the boys, who you know are all different inside in the way they approach things—trying to settle each of you in there as snugly as I can. Frederick and William can start standing on their own feet. Frederick will work with me, and William's already talking about setting himself up in a produce store. Ed says there are excellent schools for Walter and John. I'll be as anxious as you to make new friends. We can write to Annie every day if you want."

He turned to look out the window to get his bearings. He was intimately familiar with every inch of the country they passed through. *Didn't I survey this very line?*

He pulled at the watch-chain stretched across his waist.

"Look, all you lads, we are approaching the last station before beginning our climb to the switchback. The views of the countryside and mountains from it are fantastic."

Twenty-three

In Newcastle's Tighe's Hill, on Maitland Road, Martha and Charles together found a large bungalow, so new they could choose paint colours and wallpapers. The grounds offered a spacious front garden with a gazebo and, at back, stables large enough to house a gig, a sulky and three horses—with a back-lane exit. Charles paid a large deposit and signed a contract for regular monthly instalments against the balance.

Ed and Maggie Bourn had arranged 'Sunday tea' in their Hamilton garden on the Richardson's first weekend, its purpose to offer help in orientating the newcomers. Ed in fact appointed the wife of one of his staff to introduce Martha to markets and stores in respect of everything from foodstuffs to clothing and furniture. Maggie recalled how ignorant one felt when arriving in a new environment.

Ed and Charles sat on a veranda smoking pipes while Maggie and Martha were comfortable in their garden's gazebo.

Frederick, Martha couldn't help but notice, was deep in conversation with Edie Bourn under an apple tree, while William walked the gardens with Edie's sister, Hope.

"My name is also Martha," Maggie admitted. "However, it was also my mother's name, so I was called Maggie. And it stayed."

"Oh, what a coincidence," whispered Martha Richardson, "and the coincidence of both our husbands being railway men."

"Another is that both families made the journey out within month of each other."

"And both boarding ship with small children at heel, Maggie."

"And both giving birth in the South Atlantic, Martha."

"And both being daughters."

They touched on nothing other than such innocent incidents. If they were to become close friends, close enough to share more personal moments of their lives, propriety demanded that time must engineer it.

The men were also establishing greater rapport. They had the advantage of having met—a meeting to instil respect in each for the other.

"That we can scratch each other's back in adopting our new town together, Charles, is a welcome benefit for each your advantage, and mine. The quicker I can help settle you in, the sooner you and Frederick can start work. Can you, as early as tomorrow, come to my office to look at the layout of the city? Is your William up to helping his mother do the settling in, that Frederick can accompany you?"

"Frederick and I will make time, Ed. I shall want, at your convenience, one of your fellows to drive Frederic and me around that we can see the layout's terrain—exactly where you have line extensions and stations in mind. We have our own instruments."

"The line is pretty much there. However, I feel minor changes will help service the community. And yes, we need to establish where to build stations that the line can be used for local commuting as well as freight. Frederick has qualifications?"

"Fully qualified. I taught him myself, so can vouch for his prowess." Charles looked about. "I saw him a little while ago—walking with one of your daughters, and William with another."

Ed smiled. "I've plenty to go around."

"My only one we left in Bathurst. You may recall I wanted to wait for her wedding. Martha was sad at leaving her, of course, her being an only daughter."

"Separating from family is something all immigrants suffer. Bathurst is not that far, however. Your parents, yours and Martha's, are they still alive in the old country?"

"Some. I have a mother in Northampton City. Martha's mother is in Brixworth. She had recent news of her father's death."

"A sad time when too far away to share grief with kin. Maggie and I had each lost both parents before leaving, yet both had many siblings to farewell. My father was a coach-builder for the railways—that's how I was inducted."

"And what about food in this land, Ed? A man never saw lamb back there that he can here eat every day of the week, lamb to render English mutton tasteless."

"Oh yes. And the beef? Never could we find beef there that one could eat both rare and tender."

Charles was pleased to find Ed anxious to get to work. An impatient streak had ever been a characteristic—fortunately a cautious impatience. To get on with whatever work beckoned had become instinctive.

~ * ~

Three months later

On her fiftieth birthday, Martha inspected her body in her long mirror. She had been developing a roundness over recent years.

"I shall start dieting, Charles."

They sat on their veranda as Sybil, the housemaid, washed the dinner dishes.

Martha having hinted, with sufficient notice, that her fiftieth birthday was looming, Charles actually sounded her out, having given it a few day's thought, on employing a housemaid in honour of such a significant birthday. Martha had been chuffed, of course.

"But I shall still do my own marketing and cooking. This is a big house, and she will have enough to do with that, as well as laundry."

She then sighed before adding, "Oh, how I shall miss having to do the laundry of now four working men in the family!"

He smiled at the pert set of her lips as she sat back.

"It will give you more time to maybe exercise, my dear, instead of dieting?"

"I must diet. Look how tall and slim Maggie is. And she would be about my age—slim after bearing nine children when I had only five! I shall stop eating breads and puddings."

"Wheat is a healthy food, girl, and sugar gives energy. Anyway, I like to see you happy, and you wouldn't look happy if hungry. So be sensible about your diet."

He leaned close. "Anyway, I like a little spare flesh around your waist—it's nice for a man to grip on to when giving you a squeeze. It increases cuddling pleasure tenfold."

She giggled and slapped his hand.

She never began her diet. She preferred the extra thrill she now got every time he put his arm around her. *A little fatness,* she decided, *is maybe, then, something to enjoy.*

But I do miss my Annies. Arthur's Annie is my oldest friend here, and I miss her natural honesty. She never drew lines in what I call prudish behaviour, rather could say what was in her mind, delicate to strange ears or not. I learned to value that. Our own Annie's special warmth, I put down to her being an only daughter, of course. I guess I will forever keep wondering if she is all right.

"Have you noticed, Charles, how quickly our Annie answers most of our letters? I worry less, that way, but it just makes me worry more when there is a longer than usual gap."

"Maybe some of yours don't reach her. Mail from Bathurst, I read in the *Herald*, is frequently robbed by highwaymen. Cobb & Co. has reverted to guards riding shotgun. The villains abscond with mail-bags in the hope of finding gold-dust being mailed to outlying families."

"That's only mail going west, Charles. Inward mail comes by train, not by stage."

Charles slapped his own wrist. *A man can't admit such a failing in words, of course. It only invites her to think on my weak points.*

Yet he felt no guilt. He considered it a man's privilege to insist on his family seeing him a step ahead of all. *Especially the women!*

We've the old queen to thank for that, of course, setting examples for women to consider themselves at least equal. Yet nor can we put that into bloody words!

So he smiled. "Yes, dear, of course!"

Neither did she follow it up. She was the first to recognise his "Of course," answer as a tacit victory. Instead, she reverted to her usual ploy of changing the subject.

"Have you noticed how frequently William walks out with Hope Bourn? I'm beginning to think he is shrewdly manoeuvring opportunities. Surely you've noticed it's always him wanting to deliver your messages to Ed. And why should every occasion take several hours when they live so close?"

"Of course I've noticed it. Only time he was back within thirty minutes was when Hope was at the theatre with Rosa and Edie. But there might be a short reprieve on all that. Ed told me 'several of his girls' had made a last-minute decision to join Rosa for a shopping trip in Sydney."

"Who's looking after Rosa's children, then? I'm surprised she would leave them with Bill. Or has he gone, too? Surely Maggie wouldn't let the girls go unescorted. And where will they stay in Sydney?"

Charles laughed aloud.

"I don't know, to your first question. Nor about the second. Or third. Nor am I really interested. I'm quite sure both Maggie and Ed are responsible enough to have covered all angles, including Rosa's children."

"Hhhh!"

Charles, no longer taking long absences, was beginning to realise how great a difference he was finding domestic life. During all his married life, he had been away for periods of several weeks—even months when 'Up the Grose' and 'On the switchback.' Being now constantly home of an evening, he was finding himself confronted with such mediocre problems as why another family might choose to do this or that without Martha being consulted. It amused him that she considered such things important.

Yet not enough to dare pursue them!

~ * ~

Early the following year

"Thank heavens you will soon be off our hands, Hope," Ed joked. "Your dear mama and me are counting the days to, to… When is it again, your wedding?"

Hope kissed him on the brow.

"November, Papa. William insists he needs time to get his business established so he can keep me 'in the custom he wishes to illustrate.' And I do not want it to seem I'm trying to pressure him."

Ed tilted his chin high and stared down his nose.

"Oh, dear. Here are your Mama and me desperately anxious to cast off all you demanding daughters so we can enjoy life again, and you all seem to be taking forever about it. Only Rosa married and gone when we had been hoping for more. And you, Edie, our other daughter with hooks into these poor Richardson lads—what plans have you and Frederick? You pay him so much attention, surely the thought of marriage has crossed your minds. Or are you going to disappoint us also?"

Not only Edie and Hope but all the sisters were by now giggling at their father's antics. Maggie simply sat with her crochet, a bemused smile on her lips.

"We have indeed talked on marriage in the future, Papa," Edie said once her own giggles subsided. "Possibly two years from now. Freddie doesn't want to interfere with my career. His attitude is that in marriage, both should concentrate on blessing the marriage with early children. And such would certainly mean the end of my career."

Edie possessed a delightfully rich contralto voice, unusual in one of such slight physique, and was in great demand as an entertainer. She performed not only at concerts staged by the city, but at private after-dinner functions and at weddings and funerals. It was a career that would certainly be at risk once beginning a family. Her statement, however, had a startling effect on the moment's frivolity.

All giggling stopped. Maggie even paused her needle, the hand remaining aloft. It seemed to freeze as if in an ice storm, awaiting some signal before resuming. Ed cocked his bowed head to one side, peering at Edie from under his bushy eyebrows. Her five sisters had mouths all but agape.

"Are you saying, Edie, that you and Frederick have discussed such an intimate subject?"

"Yes, Papa, on several occasions. But only since he received your permission to propose. And proposing means marriage. And marriage means begetting children, Papa..."

The younger girls, Maude and Emily, now thirteen and nine years, put their hands to their mouths, quite in awe at Edie speaking so forwardly before the entire family.

"We discuss things openly, Papa. He is a modern man and recognises my similar attitudes. We find it a satisfying bonding."

Ed came to Edie and put his arm around her waist.

"Your dear mama and me," he said, addressing all the daughters, "certainly set out to raise our children with modern outlooks. We believe that observing the tight confines of propriety that convention insists on should not restrict husbands and wives from being frank with each other. We are the first to believe strong bonds are better woven by addressing our personal lives openly."

He turned towards Maggie. "So, my dear wife... I think our daughter has illustrated that we have achieved some success."

Maggie laid down her crochet and crossed her hands in her lap.

"Yes, my dear. However I think neither of us expected a daughter to begin exercising such a controversial freedom before marriage."

She looked over the tops of her *pince-nez* at her Edie, still clasped by her father. "Has this free attitude with Frederick extended to physical contact, Edie?"

The younger sisters, and even Hope, Eliza, and Jessie, showed instant alarm.

Edie was visibly shocked.

"No, Mama. Certainly not! We have kissed on numerous occasions, although politely so. And I hope he will forgive me for telling this to you all. But he does realise that my parents have a more modern outlook than others. He has a similar rapport with his father, he has told me. He insists his mother is 'not yet ready for it.' However, his father is forever wagging a finger at both Freddie and William, I am told, to observe rules of etiquette with all daughters, those of the Bourns in particular. So, my darling parents, that is where my relationship with Freddie starts and finishes, other than that I love him very much."

She made her point with a beaming smile on her face. "However I am the first to admit I am as anxious as Hope in looking forward to my day of marriage."

Hope ran to her and threw her arms around her sister.

"And I notice you are calling him Freddie, Edie dear. Do you think his family will be happy with that?"

"I know not. I am content in that he enjoys it."

There were several years between Edie and Hope, Edie coming up twenty-one and Hope not due to turn eighteen until several months before her marriage. Yet their aspirations towards their futures fell along parallel lines.

Maggie, however, retook the floor. "Another thing we are fortunate about in respect of our daughters is that you all have grown up with a healthy sense of comradeship. Can I ask that both Edie and Hope liaise with the rest of you, in the immediate future, to gather amongst yourselves that, both within the context of propriety yet without the confines of Victorian prudery, you can instruct other girls on the values they recognise? I am sure it would prove considerably more meaningful than coming from me. Do you understand what I am asking? And why?"

"Young Maude and Emily, too?" asked Ed.

"Indeed, my dear. We are simply one big, enlightened family with a more sensible outlook on life than our dear Sovereign. Methinks she would be more worldly if she didn't cosset her morals in a such a tight little cocoon."

Twenty-four

Charles Frederick Richardson sat with his father in the privacy of Charles' study.

Frederick was anxious to marry his Edie yet was determined not to do so until seeing a clearer path to a secure future.

"Edie calls you Freddie. You happy with that?"

"Yes, Pa. She likes it, so I like it."

"Your sister Annie's husband is called Freddie. It seems a habit in this country to shorten names. Would you rather be a Freddie here at home also, rather than being Freddie in one place and Frederick in another?"

"If you and Ma are happy with that, I certainly would be."

"Well, boy, your ma and I have discussed it, and decided you should choose. You're the one bearing the name. So that makes you Freddie, from here on, eh?"

They both, by this time, were smiling.

"Yes please, Pa. I've liked it ever since Edie coined it for me."

"Then Freddie it is, boy. But it's not only that, I wanted to talk with you. There is the more meaty subject of your future. I know you've been anxious to talk on it."

Freddie breathed a great sigh. "Yes, indeed, Pa. Edie's and my future depend on it."

Charles knocked his pipe out in the ashtray, pulled his tobacco pouch from its pocket in his waist-coat, and began filling it.

"Let's start with Ed Bourn. You already realise he works to a pretty tight timetable, I'd reckon?"

Freddie nodded. "Indeed."

"And he keeps the pressure on me to meet it, just as much as he does on all who answer to him. Most of the team is away in bivouacs, and he's been pulling strings to keep you and me still working from home, yet he is running out of time on that. And I've reached the stage of looking forward to getting back to carpentry. I've had enough of bivouac living. I'm going to move into the carriage shop for the four or five years before I retire."

Freddie was itchy. He too, was anxious about foreseeing his own five-year programme. *When is Pa going to get around to* my *future?*

Charles was just back from New England, checking progress on the Great Northern Line's new 'stretch.' Government policy was that immediately after surveys for each 'next' stretch, the line between the planned next two stations was complete, track-layers would be right on their heels laying tracks. So each 'stretch' was a programme all its own: route planned, survey complete, tracks laid, stations built, train services begun to that forward station.

Behind it, not only were tracks already being laid for the next 'stretch,' but surveyors were already a 'stretch' beyond it again. Building a railroad was a never-ending series of repeat operations.

Things were currently in limbo because with trains already running to the foot of the New England Plateau, finding a path up the steep incline was proving difficult. It wasn't a case of tunnels; here it was simply a case of how-steep-the-grades. The range here was so wide that to try to go around the impasse would add several hundred miles to the line. Already there was a roadway cut, but in many areas it was too steep for a railroad. Considerable earthworks had been decided on—cutting and filling—and this was causing the delay in completing this vital 'stage.' Branch-lines were being built elsewhere, whilst the earthworks up to the plateau proceeded. Engineers and surveyors had to be working hand in hand constructing every mile. Charles had been spending much time on site, working with the engineers.

Freddie's life was totally wrapped around the railways, and he was beginning to realise that if he and Edie were to marry, they would have to put up with him working away from home for some time. The path Edie wanted, of course, was having him at home.

Yet her father wasn't easy to sway. He was dedicated to his responsibilities, and that meant personnel should be simply at beck and call according to their skills.

"Freddie will have to spend time away from home until he has earned a more administrative position," Edie had been told. "He's been trained by his father in surveying and is highly skilled. Yet he still needs field experience before given more responsibility. He is a bright lad, destined for a worthwhile career. But this is government work, and one must follow procedures."

Ed had suggested to Charles that he should talk it through with Freddie.

"I cannot play favourites, Charles. I'm the first to realise the lad is not looking for that as much as is Edie. In fact he is the one to help me straighten Edie out. And you are the one to tell him so, because it is you he reports to. I cannot have her continually hinting things at me."

Charles agreed.

"My problem is, Pa, I don't want to be living in 'away' bivouacs when my little ones are growing up. I know you had to, and I'm not complaining about that because you've ended up giving us all a comfortable home—one highly appreciated. But growing up without a father at home is not what I want for my sons. Edie is a well-educated young woman, and we live in a city with theatres and sophisticated entertainment. For her to continue enjoying those things once married, she needs a husband for escort. I want to share those things with her."

Charles took his time lighting his pipe.

"They're fine sentiments, lad. And I'd like to think you can do all that. That's what we're here to talk about. But for the next five years,

Ed reckons, you've to 'go through channels,' and that means working away in bivouacs. If you want to work with the railways, you can take the road Walter has his eyes on. He's already told me wants to be a station master when he grows up. But that too is going to mean accepting transfers through country towns before such a career can lead to Newcastle Central, for instance. Everything to do with railways, boy, is travel, unless you want a job on a machine in a workshop. It's a take-it-or-leave-it situation. Why can't you and Edie do what your ma and I did? Live in married-quarters bivouacs? Many of the lads are doing it."

Freddie's eyes sought the carpet. "Edie has grown up in a home on high living with housemaids and cooks and gardeners and—"

Charles put up a staying hand.

"Maybe you must stop thinking about marriage, lad, if Edie is not prepared to take you as your ma took me. Marriage is a two-person thing. If Edie wants you, she must live the life her man can give her. I came up through the ranks and can now afford to give my family benefits my father couldn't give me. Your ma had to take the bad with the good. She was a Burgess..." He held his hand up again while he walked to his bookshelf and took the dictionary from its shelf.

"Look at this..."

burgess, n. borough citizen with civic station — member of parliament, borough leader, university dean...

"Your grandmother was high-born in Brixworth Manor, boy, the same big house your ma lived in when I met her, but her ma married a low-born peasant and lived the low-born life because in those days it was one or the other. And she made a happy home to raise your ma in. You and me, boy, are middle class. And so is Edie. Just that her pa happened to work in the railway industry when it boomed to the extent that it changed the world. He was caught up in that surge. The steam-engine began the industrial revolution that spilled my pa out on the scrap-heap of those not so lucky. Ed's done well. He's an astute man, so I'm not begrudging him his luck. And in this new land with so much growth and potential, any man with some education can do well. I can't give you answers on how to get instant riches—I've given you the education for facing your future from a catapult rather than you flapping elbows as the uneducated must do, hoping they can gain enough momentum to become air-born. So now you've got to plot your own course. You need a wife who will follow you. It's up to you and Edie to work out how you do that."

Freddie was quiet for a long time. Charles could see his disappointment, but what he was saying had to be said.

"I guess I've to assume, Pa, in respect of me being home while my boys grow up, is that the worst situation is that a babe arrives in our first year of marriage. But then if we don't marry for say two years, then he'd be two or three by the time I'm through my fieldwork and can live at home. Edie will have to be content with that."

Charles didn't see the need for congratulating his son on seeing sense.

"And it's up to only you, boy, to make sure you are the first of your team to get the promotions as they come up—so you're the quicker back 'indoors.' I've the experience to help you, but there will be study involved. Engineering progresses are coming along by leaps and bounds, so you'll have to keep up with it. Edie's pa can help in pointing you in the right directions as he sees changes in the making. He thinks well of you, that's obvious. You can always insist she comes to live in bivouac with you until you've earned an 'at home' job. She must cut her cloth according to what life you can afford to give her."

They chatted on until Freddie felt he had enough advice to work on. He had it made clear that both his own pa and Edie's were of like minds on it, and Edie and he did indeed have to realise they must find their own way around the impasse.

When Charles was satisfied Freddie fully realised he would have support of both fathers if taking the hard line with Edie, he stood, placing a hand on Freddie's shoulder.

"I'm going to make cocoa for your ma now, lad. You want one?"

Freddie stood, smiling. "I'll help you."

They found Martha sitting with her elbows on the kitchen table, hands cupping her chin.

"Yes, I'd love a cup, please. Just put it there," she said, moving one hand to tap the table.

"What are you reading, girl?"

"Charles Darwin again. I loaned it to Maggie, and she gave it back to me yesterday. I'm finding it more meaningful the second time around. It must be what, ten years since reading it?" She giggled. "Or should I say 'struggled through it?' My reading's come a long way since then."

When cocoa was made and Charles had re-introduced her son Frederick to her as Freddie, at which she smiled and pulled his head down for a kiss, Freddie took his cup off to sit and cogitate on his next meeting with Edie.

Charles sat beside Martha and gently pushed the green-bound volume aside. "Just leave Mr. Darwin for a minute, Mother, while I fill you in on my chat with Freddie."

"It seems strange, him suddenly becoming Freddie. He was happy about it, I take it?"

"Indeed. I got the feeling he was quite chuffed that Edie dubbed it on him."

"And his work situation?"

"He's at a life's crossroad, of course—trying to sort his mind around things. You know Ed offered to move me into the carriage shop when I felt ready for it?"

She nodded.

"Well, I might just do that sooner rather than later. I'm thinking of asking Ed if, with my help in the background, Fred is up to taking over from me in the field. That would be a sort of short-cut, if Ed thinks he's ready."

"Oh, yes. And you working indoors all day will be a change. And a welcome one, dear."

"I'm ready for it. Out in the bloody weather at this time of year is no joy. Getting a bit long in the tooth for it now. I rather like the idea of getting back to wood-work."

"Wanting indoor work influenced William too, of course. He actually searched for an 'indoor' career—one that didn't take him away from home. What sort of fist is he making on the planning?"

"Freddy or William?"

"Well, both."

"William seems pretty sound. He has a good grasp on design—he drew for me what he already has a sign-writer making... *Wm. A. Richardson — Produce Merchant & Grain Broker*, it reads. He hasn't Freddie's grasp of people—handling people at work—although William's young yet. He will learn. A produce store is good business. And it's on a good site. There's lots of traffic up and down Blade Street, so he'll have passing traffic as well as contracting businesses on a volume-discount basis. But he'll need help with bookwork. I suggested he go to night school and learn some rudiments in accountancy, but the young blighter seems more keen to see Hope every night. After he's married, he might do a term or two. I'll keep on his back about it."

"And Frederick... Oh! Freddie, I mean?"

"He has much homework to do. If he comes back after talking with Edie with some positive sort of direction, I might just sound Ed out on me making my career move now. That would give Freddie the fillip he needs."

Twenty-five

It was raining when Martha wheeled her shopping buggy out the fishmonger's door. The Tighe's Hill High Street had butcher, grocer, greengrocer, and every ancillary shop a housewife needed to satisfy daily needs, all in close proximity.

She usually parked her gig behind the butcher-shop because he was next-door to the fishmongers. It was from these two she most wanted to get her shopping quickly home to the icebox. Baker, milkman, and iceman delivered daily so she had to shop only every second or third day. Walter, at sixteen, was in his last year of school and had lots of homework, so she no longer asked him to help with shopping. Young John was nine, the age when boys seemed to have a busier social whirl after school with friends, boys only, of course, because at that age he found girls "absolutely useless at anything!" He seemed seldom at home that he could come and help.

But rather than insist, today, with the weather looking so fine, she told him to scoot off to whatever pleasure it was that seemed so important.

But, there you go! It's the very day the weather turns cantankerous.

She looked beyond the fishmonger's back door, and there was Dobbin under a tree, patiently suffering the driving rain.

"Why can't we train them to raise the hood when it rains, so the seats are not drenched?" she asked the bemused fishmonger.

Usually when John wasn't with her, she had the boy of whichever shop was last on her list load her buggy into the gig. But not today. *I'm not driving home in this. Dobbin will have to wait.*

It was one of those storms sent solely to frustrate people—heaviest at inconvenient times. Yet she didn't mind. She settled on a chair in the shopfront where she could see when the rain eased and opened her new purchase, a little tingle of excitement fluttering around her heart. She'd just had a first-in-a-lifetime experience. She'd bought a book, a novel. When passing the newsagent's window, her attention had been sparked by a big poster by a stack of novels. *Charles Dickens' Magazine Serials Now in Novel Form*, the poster proclaimed. Several ladies were inside the store thumbing through promotional pages.

Ooh. I remember seeing those in Charles' journals. I read one chapter, but realised it was towards the end of the series. I'd missed what had gone before...

'The Pickwick Papers' was its name, I recall. And here it is in book form.

She bought it. *I believe it's something Charles might even read.*

She was so engrossed the fishmonger had to interrupt. "The rain's stopped, Mrs. Richardson. I could see you so rapt in your book you hadn't noticed..."

"Thank you, Mr. Horton. I was indeed engrossed."

She had his boy load her buggy, and she borrowed old towels to wipe down the seat.

"I shall have Sybil launder them and return them when next to market," she informed him and then drove the persevering Dobbin home.

And there was a letter from Annie to even heighten her happy day. She left the shopping for Sybil to put away and tore it open.

"Ah," she exclaimed aloud. "I am a grandma! My first grandchild. A little Emily!"

There was no one to hear her other than Sybil. And Walter in his bedroom doing homework. At least he rushed in.

"And that makes you an uncle, Walter. What do you think of that?"

She was now anxious for Charles to arrive home, to give him both her snippets of news.

~ * ~

William Richardson, a handsome lad of twenty-three, was the pride and joy of both Martha and Charles at his marriage. Newcastle City's *St. Johns* was aglitter with the city's social set. The Bourn family moved in elegant circles.

Martha wore her first ever 'tailored' costume. The matching hat and gloves made her feel like a million pounds. Charles had been fitted for his first suit of 'tails.'

"I'm going to have to keep in trim, Mother, so it will still fit for Freddie and Edie's wedding."

"And for those of Hope's four unmarried sisters?"

"Bloody likely," he whispered in her ear.

"And William! I notice Hope is persistently, of a sudden, calling him 'Will.' Do you think this means we, too, should be shortening his name?"

Charles laughed. "Maybe I shall have to sound him out on that."

After three days in Sydney for their honeymoon, Will, as he began to be regularly called hence by all at home, and Hope took a rented house in Hamilton, close to her parents.

Straight after the wedding, however, Martha received another letter from Annie.

She opened it with glee—avid for news of her granddaughter.

But she dropped the letter, watched it flutter its way to the floor so she could clasp her hands to her mouth. Little Emily had died.

"The doctors don't know why," Annie explained. "She had shown no signs of illness. She was just dead in her cot one morning."

When Charles arrived home, Martha was still distraught.

"Oh, Charles—how I need to be with her! We hear about these unexplained cot deaths, but there's never been one as close to home as this. And her first little one..."

"Sad indeed, Mother. I'd intended writing her, anyway, to tell her about Will's wedding. But maybe you should do that. Tell her—"

"I shall write—to tell her I'm coming to Bathurst!" Martha stamped her foot. "She must feel the loneliest person in the world, there all alone. And if I tell her I am coming, that will take her mind off her loneliness even if not her grief. Can you get some money from the bank for me, Charles? I shall write now, and you can post it when by the bank."

Charles was astounded.

"You've never travelled alone. You are going to need an overnight in Sydney while you get a train ticket, and that means a hotel. And how will you manage with your luggage?"

"I don't need help, Charles. I will manage. You just see if I don't!"

He had never seen her with such an air of determination.

"Take young Walter with you. He can look after your baggage and run messages for you. I will feel happier if he is with you..."

"Walter should not miss school. I shall manage perfectly well."

But Charles couldn't be satisfied. "Women don't go traipsing around countrysides alone. It just isn't done. I will worry about you every minute."

"If you had greater faith in me, you would worry less!"

Oh, oh! Time to bloody back off. She's really rattling her shackles on this one.

"Well, at least do this for me—let me right now sit down and work out how much money you'll need. And I'll give you extra so you can give it to Annie. There are many expenses in a funeral, even for such a little tot. And I'll write to the Great Southern Hotel in Sydney—it's close to the station, and reserve a room for you. I don't want you traipsing around the town looking for accommodation. And I'll ask Ed to give you a note to the station master. He'll ensure you get a seat and see you get help with luggage. And a letter to Annie will only arrive a day or so before you, so we should send a telegram."

He had to smile, then, for Martha was making tea.

"Thank you for all that, dear. We shall both have tea while we plan what is to be done. I have taken that train trip several times, you know. I went from Bathurst to Parramatta to have young John, you might recall. And I had both the train and the steamer getting here."

"But you weren't alone, Mother. And you've never had to seek accommodation in a strange town—and you are not really familiar with Sydney. When I go to the bank I'll also get you a berth for the steamer. An overnight one will be best. It will be too tiring if you take the morning steamer—it could then be supper-time before you get to your hotel. On the night run, meals are easier for a traveller to organise. Ed has found that is the best way of doing it."

Martha was half listening. Her mind was on what clothes she had that didn't first need laundering. She wanted to get to Annie with the least delay. And she had to sit with Sybil to make sure the family would get fed properly during her absence. Martha now had a laundress come in one day a week, while Sybil lived in to clean the house and prepare some dishes towards Martha's cooking. Martha would never trust house-help to cook for her family... "But I find it a help when she can do some of the time-consuming things like shelling peas and peeling pumpkin," she would tell Maggie.

Martha and Sybil got on well.

"It's because of my time at the Brixworth Manor," she told Charles. "I learned, then, how to keep on the right side of staff."

And whilst I've done much travelling since, she told her alter-ego, *this will be my first opportunity of not simply 'following my leader.'*

She felt quite smug in looking forward to being her own boss while 'on the road.'

Twenty-six

"You know, Annie, even though I enjoyed the independence of travelling alone, near every minute of it, I never stopped wondering how the family is faring—if they're eating well—even worrying if they're getting enough. And if Sybil's coping all right with the shopping. I like to make my own choices when it comes to fruit and vegetables. And steak."

Annie giggled. She was not only ecstatic that her ma had come, but intrigued at her doing it alone.

"And you had no trouble, Ma, getting your train ticket, for instance? And how did you cope with your luggage? It's surely more than you could carry."

"There are always porters for first-class passengers, dear. And the higher you hold your chin, I learned, the quicker they flock to you. When the steamer docked, a porter followed with a trolley to where hansoms queued. He loaded everything. Then the hotel's porter unloaded. I never had to carry a thing."

"You knew where to go for your train ticket?"

"No. Our friend Mr. Bourn gave me a letter addressed to the station master at Redfern, and I simply tipped the hotel porter tuppence to deliver it for me. He came back with the ticket, and this morning, for another tuppence, he drove me in the hotel's own gig and delivered everything up to a railway porter."

"How'd you know how to do all that?"

"By watching your father, dear. We came all the way from England, with not only several times as much baggage but with your two big brothers. They weren't big, then of course, young enough to be still running off to inspect this and that strange sight if I didn't clasp them tightly by the hand."

Martha liked Annie's Freddie. He was a quiet young man, of slight build. Yet he had a cough Martha was uneasy about.

"He's developed it only since we married, Ma. He jokes that it must be my cooking. But it comes and goes."

They talked into the night, Martha telling them much of Newcastle, how many more facilities were available than in rural Bathurst.

"And the salt air, when living by the sea, Annie, lends a healthy sort of vigour to the atmosphere. I was surprised, once having left it, to realise how used to it I had become."

Martha would retire each night for the week she stayed content that she no longer had to face the unknown future that weighed so heavily on the younger generation. She felt so content with her life that her placid mind proved enough solace to despatch her quickly asleep.

~ * ~

Ed Bourn felt stretched for time. Inspector of Rolling Stock encompassed the overall responsibilities of establishing standards and safety procedures, locomotive and carriage design, supply contracts, the entire manufacturing operations, and stock maintenance. He was, in effect, chief engineer of all mechanical operations. As such a senior executive, he was under pressure to relocate to Sydney that he was on-site for people like the transport minister and the chief of 'Everleigh,' the entire continent's biggest railway engineering workshop—a location move he was continuing to resist.

He was being 'ground down' trying to make more holes in the top of the pepper pot his job had become. In Newcastle, he was currently working with architects on the city's most adventurous Victorian building edifice, the Royal Newcastle Station. Directly opposite the impressive Customs House, it was to be the city's most impressive landmark. Everything about it had to be 'just-bloody-right!'

And in Sydney, the NSW Government Railways were trying to erect more workshop buildings with Ed in distant Newcastle. He was being pressured from many angles. His timetable for completion of new line sections, which meant new stations being built as the spider-legs of lines spread through an area four times the size of Great Britain, had his mind boggling.

Oh, had I ever envisaged anything like this when I left England?

And he had a large family to oversee.

Thank God I have a wife of outstanding education and ability to grasp challenges and cope with them!

Private railways still ran from collieries to the Hexham wharves. He was happy to leave those outside his areas of responsibility—other than to criticize them if their operation was hindering his own work

So long as they think the government might monopolize them, they will jump to attention when I complain. So as long as they respond to my needling, I am saved that additional responsibility. And now I'm to lose Charles' keen eyes in the field. But I can't deny him wanting to start winding down.

I simply need more middle-men behind me instead of having to do so much myself.

Oh, how I wish I had sons!

~ * ~

Three months after Martha's return, Walter finished school. He began working for the railway. Ed took the lad into his own office so he could get a feel of how administration worked.

"If you are your father's son, lad, you have the makings of senior management. He tells me you have a yen to be a station-master?"

"Oh, yes sir."

So Walter's career path was established.

And Martha received another letter from Annie.

"I am pregnant again, Ma. And have hardly been sick at all. And we are leaving Bathurst. Freddie has been offered a job in Forbes— seventy miles west of here, but the train now reaches Forbes and even beyond."

"West of Bathurst, Charles? So she is even further away?"

"If a man's work takes him, Mother, she must follow. Same as us leaving England. And we, too, left Bathurst to move on, didn't we?"

"But we came to a larger town, Charles. Annie is now in an even smaller town."

~ * ~

Freddie was visiting the Bourns at Hamilton, but not on this occasion to see Edie. Ed had summoned him. They sat in his study.

"Edie keeps pestering me about your prospects, lad. And your worthy father tells me he has talked with you about it. All this comes at a time when every rail executive in the colony is finding himself under pressure with lines now under construction in every direction, constituents even in outlying areas besieging their sitting members to more quickly have railway lines servicing their district. And right here, lad, I need help. I am employing more administrative staff in the hope some will quickly develop management skills..."

Freddie was anxious, waiting for Edie's pa to get to his own prospects.

"...You have already illustrated your potentials throughout my family, Freddie, so I have thoughts as to your future. But progress must still take its course. Your father is moving aside, he tells me. And he has asked that you might be included among those being considered for that position..."

Fred was trying desperately not to let his mouth suddenly beam in a wide smile.

"...However!"

Oh oh!

"...There is more than one option to be considered for your future. I am as keen as you, lad, to see you marry my Edie and be able to provide a good life for her. However, executive positions must mature over time. Apples on even a flourishing tree must begin as a bud and mature under the right conditions. I am in a position to envisage the growth of this railway industry of ours with increasing accuracy—and I see our greatest problem is growth with insufficient skills to keep our apple-tree growing healthily. We are importing skills from England because we haven't the experience needed here. But of course we risk acquiring only those who haven't yet illustrated value to British Rail they are prepared to see them depart. Do you get my gist?"

Fred wasn't yet quite sure.

If it's local skills he must otherwise insist on, he's already said there are insufficient available.

"It's working its way through, sir."

Ed smiled.

"We need to begin training future executives here. We realise our greatest lack is experienced inspectors. And tomorrow we are going to need even more than today. It is on the inspectors' shoulders that top executives delegate responsibilities in the various operational areas. I am Inspector of Rolling Stock. We also have inspectors in other facets of operation. I believe you have the mettle, Freddie, of becoming an inspector. There are several levels in reaching it, and each requires specialist training. In Sydney, recognising tomorrow's need, training courses are currently being established. We shall have a branch here. Are you now closer to getting my gist?"

"Absolutely, sir."

"I would like to suggest you do not yet take over your father's role. I would like to first see you with more experience in leadership. I am appointing a more senior man, with experience, to take that role. He will be responsible for surveys on all branches of the Great Northern Line, but I would hope you will begin as an assistant to him. It will carry its own responsibilities, and as you will realise, these are increasing in number as each hundred miles of line is laid. So coming back to my apple-tree—the more branches it gets, the more buds for ripening fruit will develop. Promotion for the right men will be quick."

Fred was feeling far happier. He let his future father-in-law see him smile.

"Just to give you a feel for what I'm talking about, Freddie, the current wage for a wagon builder is nine shillings per day. For a wagon examiner, twelve shillings a day. For an engine-driver first-class, thirteen shillings a day. For an inspector, seventeen shillings a day. If you wish to now go away and think on all that, and decide to follow such a course, advise your father."

~ * ~

Six months later, another letter arrived from Annie. *I have a son, Ma. We named him William. All is well, and we like Forbes.*

At home, Freddie Richardson had accepted the role of assistant to the chief of surveys, appointed not only to the Great Northern Line as Charles, for the time being, remained, but to all New South Wales Lines. His several assistants were delegated to overseeing the several lines under construction in the colony.

"A clear indication of the growth Ed talked about," he explained to Charles.

"Give me another year tutoring you into the role, boy, then I'll move to the carriage shop."

Freddie could almost hear his pa and Ed Bourn working that one out between them.

"Now it's up to me to respond," he told Edie. "I reckon we can start thinking about marriage when that happens."

"Well, please make it happen soon, darling. I have faith in you, you know."

~ * ~

A year later, another letter from Annie. *Terrible news that I hate having to write to you. Not only is little Billy dead, but also I lost Freddie. I have just buried him. I feel so frightened and alone.*

Charles wasted no time. Next day he went to the bank and withdrew £20, tucked it into an envelope with a note, and posted it off, registered mail.

The letter said:

> Pack your clothes, girl, and arrange to freight on everything else. Two weeks from the day you receive this

letter, quit your house and take the train to Sydney. Book
yourself into The Great Southern Hotel and wait there for
Walter, who will come to bring you here.

"Get yourself organised, son," he told nineteen-year-old Walter.
"Go fetch your sister home."

He put an arm about the distraught Martha.

"You see, Mother, she's not so far away. Soon she'll be back with
us. We will have our daughter home again."

Martha smiled. *This man is indeed my knight in shining armour.
I continue to realise my luck in meeting him—to get luckier still when
he fell in love with me. I love even his faults.*

They despatched Walter off on his errand of mercy and sat
impatiently waiting for their daughter to arrive home.

Twenty-seven

In Newcastle, Annie received the warmest welcome any daughter could hope for.

Yet the family was amazed to find her bulgingly pregnant.

"Little Billy died with the whooping cough," she told them. "Freddie had a slow and painful death from tuberculosis. I didn't tell you about that because I didn't want you worrying about me."

They hugged her closely and rearranged rooms in the house. With Will now gone, Freddie moved into what had been Charles' study, and Charles had a builder enclose part of the veranda as his new workplace.

And when her boy was born, Annie named him Walter after the brother who came to her aid.

Martha was thrilled to have a new baby in the house.

"It's made me feel twenty years younger," she told Maggie.

~ * ~

Newcastle was becoming an even more buoyant city. In each succeeding year, tonnages of coal shipped from the port increased enormously as new seams continued to be found right through the Hunter Valley. Population passed the ten thousand mark. Both families were exuberant when the suburb of Hamilton was proclaimed the 'best laid out and most attractive' suburb. It was also declared the most popular—"despite the train fare to the city costs tuppence."

Freddie married his Edie at St. Johns. They became what Martha termed 'a deliriously happy couple,' renting a house in nearby Wickham's Charlton Street. Edie gave up her career, at least temporarily, when falling pregnant. Yet that didn't work well for them. They named the boy Walter, but the tot was not to survive. He died soon after birth.

Will and Hope named their firstborn Charles Frederick. Was there any doubt he might grow up to a lifetime career in the railway?

One of the dimmest lowlights, however, struck all as time was to indicate the seriousness of Maggie's listlessness and generally failing health. The best doctors not only in Newcastle but also in Sydney's Macquarie Street were of the opinion she suffered from a cancer in either her stomach or intestines. Both families realised it only a matter of time. They could only look to a future of sadly watching their dear Maggie deteriorate.

Young John Richardson moved from home to board with Will and Hope. He worked for Will in the produce store.

Walter Richardson was appointed assistant station master at West Maitland in the Hunter Valley, what was to become the 'Crewe' of the colony's railway system—in this case a junction of four lines. Walter married there, his entire family, of course, travelling the fifteen miles for the occasion to see him wed his Ann.

~ * ~

Ed Bourn's delaying tactics on his transfer to Sydney were not sufficiently strong to defy what became a demand. In 1880, he collected his three unmarried daughters, for Eliza was already in Sydney, married but a year since, and his ailing Maggie around him, and shipped to the colony's capital.

"It had to come," he explained to the broader family. "I won several years' reprieve, but pressure became an edict."

He was loathe to be moving Maggie from her home of twenty-five years. "But at least, my dear, we shall be close to Macquarie Street."

Macquarie Street was the stately boulevard in Sydney's city where the most worthy of the continent's medical profession had their clinics.

He purchased a property, one of a newly developed terrace of gracious homes in Sydney's Chippendale. Number 40 Rose Street was so close to the Government Railway's Everleigh Workshop that Ed could walk to it in one direction, as he could to the big *Bon Marché* department store in the other. It was roomy enough to house his three daughters, two housemaids, a cook, and a gem of a widow, Susannah Ford, whose sole function was to be companion for, and to provide every personal assistance to, Maggie. Maggie herself chose Susannah from the many applicants.

The Bourn departure, however, created a massive gap in the Richardsons' social and family life. Yet even in what was left of that, the heavenly clouds were darkening—beginning to cluster for another major storm.

~ * ~

The Richardson family was to suffer two surprise deaths.

Walter lost his Ann after only a year of marriage. She died in childbirth, Walter's unborn child dying with her. And the second was even closer to home. Will, second Richardson son, husband of the still madly in love Hope, and father of four little ones, died at the young age of twenty-seven.

"It was just all so quick, Charles. I took him some broth, and he told me that what the doctor diagnosed as influenza was waning, that he expected to be up and about again within days."

Yet within another he was in hospital, and in yet another, was gone.

"How can it happen like that, Charles? I've never known anyone to be taken so quickly by influenza."

"Maybe the doctor was in error. The body is a complex thing. Even the medical profession admits to considerable ignorance of it. We read so often of new diseases, that what was yesterday thought one thing is now realised to be something new. But what it was and why, Mother, is by the way. We cannot get our Will back."

Rare tears sprang to Charles' eyes. He was cradling Martha in his arms, feeling each sob tremble through her body. Annie sat waiting. She had scooted little Walter off to play and brought a tray of tea into the parlour.

"And those darling little children, Charles. Four little mites left fatherless. What will happen there? Can we take them in here?"

Charles didn't answer. He didn't want Martha, closer to sixty than fifty, taking on that sort of responsibility. He would wait to see what happened. They knew Hope's sister Rosa had, for the nonce, left her own family and moved in with Hope to give her support and help with the littlies.

"Rosa will have telegraphed Ed," he said. "And maybe, or maybe not, he has told Maggie by now. But I doubt she could come, even though she will no doubt want to. Let's just wait until I've talked with Ed about it. Eh, girl?"

They buried their William at the nearby Waratah Cemetery.

Charles couldn't help but feel for Martha as he watched her through her black veil. They rode in the procession's lead carriage, and she had wanted to sit with her back to their direction of travel.

"I don't want to sit there, Charles, where I can see the hearse when it rounds a corner."

Freddie and Edie rode with them, Edie sitting by her ma-in-law.

Martha took a firm grasp on Edie's wrist.

"To think it was only, what, a month ago, we were all rejoicing over you naming your little one William Arthur? And Will so proud of that. Charles said to me only this morning as we were dressing that it seems a blessing, despite ironic, we still have a William Arthur in the family."

Ed and Maggie had come for the funeral. Telegrams had sped backwards and forwards arranging timings. Maggie had insisted on coming. She wanted to be with Hope, of course. They rode with Hope in the following carriage with Susannah, who was never far from Maggie's side.

Last night all had assembled for the 'wake' at the Tighe's Hill house. Will, in his casket, had been brought there rather than to his own home. Hope hadn't wanted the children, yet too young to realise what death was all about, to be confronted with it, being told their father was inside. And nor did they attend the funeral—they stayed home with their nanny.

"Huh!" Martha had said to Charles when learning Will had hired a nanny when Hope was lying-in with her fourth. "There were none around in my day. We had to get quickly out of bed and tend to our children ourselves, no matter how many there were…

"…and," she continued, "when husbands weren't even around to help. Some of us had husbands who were either 'in the field' or 'Up the Grose.'"

At which they shared a defensive little giggle.

And now this!

~ * ~

Ed and Maggie prevailed on Hope to quit the house and bring her children to Sydney.

"We have a large house with servants, so it is eminently sensible," Ed declared in almost edict style. And Hope realised how difficult, even purposeless it was in the circumstance, to stay in Newcastle. She realised she would only be a constant burden on sister Rosa.

Charles and Martha understood, although disappointed at not being able to see Will's children grow up.

"We at least get the compensation of young John moving back home, Mother."

Charles undertook the task of quitting Will and Hope's house so she could straightway leave with her parents.

"Oh, they will have such a houseful," said Martha.

"They always have had," Charles replied.

"I shall miss Hope," a tearful Edie told Freddie, "and her little ones."

"Well, we shall simply have to quickly have more of our own, my darling."

She cuddled him closely—even in public, to bring glares and stares from many.

Ed had also, whilst in Newcastle, affirmed Freddie in his new role.

"And you just let me know, Charles, when you want to move into the coach workshop."

"It will be soon, I reckon, Ed. Freddie is eager to make a success of his role, and I've had enough of field-work. Staying home is what I want for my future. I happily don't have the problem of seeing my life's partner so sadly slipping away, and I don't envy you that. But this Will thing has aged her overnight, I fear. I'm now all the more determined not to be leaving her alone. I'll be happy enough over a drawing board, or at a carpenter's bench."

The years had taught the friends to read the other like books.

"From cover to cover..." Maggie had once joked to them both.

Twenty-eight

A year later, Charles and Freddie sat in the gazebo at Tighe's Hill, sipping ales. Martha and Edie sat opposite. Edie was just out of bed, having borne little Charles Edward.

"Should we be calling him Charles or Ed?" Freddie and Edie had joked when deciding on the name. Freddie had just returned from a field visit south. It was part of his training to visit different fields.

"Soon, Pa, there'll be no need for the steamer to Sydney. There will not only be a road to Sydney but, at last, a railway. A route has been drafted. Surveyors and structural engineers will have to be holding hands during every day of the work, however. The depths of cuttings required are enormous."

"And the bridge?"

"They're already sinking footings for pylons. But it's a tortuous roadway that will be damned dangerous in the wet. The mountains are not high but extremely rugged and mostly rock, fortunately sandstone rather than granite. There's a hundred miles of road, half the entire distance of here to Sydney, all like the greatest serpentine man has ever seen."

"And the railway?"

"Immense areas of cuttings. It's been a surveyors' nightmare."

"What's the forecast?"

"Three years."

Charles whistled. "Just as well it's not granite."

~ * ~

Little Charles Edward didn't respond to the promise his given names had destined for him. He died of 'infant cholera' at four days old.

"Two babes out of three now lost, Charles. Surely those two deserve better luck."

"It's not for the want of love or nursing, Mother. I think we should feel happy that if it had to happen like this, at least Freddie was home."

So it was yet another family funeral when the tot was buried beside the Uncle Will he'd never met.

The next year Freddie and Edie rode the inaugural train to Armidale atop the New England Plateau, the halfway point of the line from Newcastle to the Queensland border. It arrived as part of the celebration opening the Armidale Railway Station. There was considerable bunting and flag-waving.

"The speech, my dearest," Freddie confided, "is the same at every new station opening. We simply change the name. Each mayor seems just as proud and pleased as the last one."

It had been a great feat getting the line up from the floor of the western plains, slow and tortuous. The New England Tableland had been a barrier to getting the road north, but a barrier now bested. Up top was a unique pocket on the Australian continent—snow fell most winters.

"Fortunately it's not snowing now. How old were you when you sailed from England?"

"Three."

"I was coming up five. So we were both too young to remember snow. I recall seeing lots of white around me at times, but that's all."

"Well, I never want to see it. I hate the cold."

"Me too."

Edie's next son they called Edward John after her father. Both prayed to heaven that he would prove a stronger child than his two brothers. He was quickly dubbed Ted, to save the problem of confusion with Ed, and prayers were answered when he thrived.

But the older generation was not as fortunate.

Charles and Martha were to lose another of their children, also at a young age.

Annie died at twenty-nine. They interred her by her brother Will.

Twenty-nine

Martha became not only grandmother but surrogate mother to young Walter Jones.

I can cope with this. Didn't I have John seven years after my own Walter? And little Walter now just ten years younger than John? That's a pretty similar age gap to have to manage. I simply have to recall the skills I used in making John feel part of his 'older' family.

Yes. I was five years behind my sister and found it enough to leave me lonely—yet little Walter is twice as far behind John. Him having been born in this very house, however, gives me the feel of him being my very own—so now it must be my role to help him through that gap.

The memory of her ma having had to bury four of her seven before a year old kept Martha more than conscious of the risks little ones had to live through to survive. It was a memory sparked every time she heard of a tot dying.

Oh, how sad it is that science cannot prevent the deaths of so many tiny ones.

But poor dear Charles. I know how devastated he is at losing his only daughter.

She tried to untangle her mind from the skills she would need to recall with young Walter, to now concentrate on Charles.

He needs a fillip. Burying our Annie on his very birthday only heightened the burden of coping with her dying so young. Fifty-eight, he turned.

Martha had already had in mind that for his sixtieth birthday she would buy him the crystal tantalus he'd so admired in David Jones.

"Just look at that, Mother. Wouldn't that look grand sitting on our sideboard? Make us feel real gentry, that would."

He'd even had the floor-walker unlock it and lift out one of its two decanters, to admire the crystal from all angles.

And the genuine silver handle and angles certainly did make it look grand.

Yes. I shall go into the city tomorrow and buy it for him now—a belated birthday present. I can always say it would be nice to have some particular thing on view, a regular reminder of our Annie. And that will help soften the blow of its cost.

So when Charles came home from work the next evening, on the sideboard sat the tantalus he'd so admired, one of its decanters filled with Scotch whisky. And after he'd got over the shock, and paid due tribute to Martha for her sentiment, he asked why only one decanter was filled.

"I didn't know what you'd want in the other, dear. I knew beer wouldn't be appropriate."

"Brandy, Mother. For when you've taken a turn. And for when Ed next visits. He enjoys a brandy after meals."

~ * ~

Hope wrote to Edie saying her father had purchased a large allotment in Sydney's Waverly cemetery. "He intends building a mausoleum so all of us who haven't willed otherwise can be buried together," she added.

And oh, how prophetic was its timing.

And of Charles' mentioning the convenience of brandy on hand for Martha.

Only a handful of months after that event was Maggie finally released from her suffering. She died at sixty-six. Ed did, then, build the mausoleum.

"If I know Ed, Martha, he knew it was getting close for Maggie. He set all this up in advance," Charles insisted.

She nodded. "Yes, he seems the inherent planner. Maggie, the poor dear, was ever sad that the only boy she gave him died so young. First of all her nine, he was."

"Strange the first two died so young when all the rest have proved so healthy."

"I hope we can say the same of Freddie and Edie. To lose two out of the first three isn't a good omen. But yes, her very parents proved that hope should never be yielded."

Ed Bourn immediately quit the Chippendale house.

It was felt in Newcastle it could have held too sad a memory for him. But less than a year later, Martha cast a wry smile.

"I wondered if maybe there was more to it than that. Edie told me while you were at work, Charles, that she has another letter from Hope. Ed slipped away and quietly married Susannah Ford, Maggie's paid 'companion.' Now what do you think of that?"

He mused for a minute or two.

"Well, all the girls are grown. Only Hope and her littlies are still 'at home'—and Ed can afford to set her up in a place of her own. So maybe he and Susannah, who, let's face it, lived in that very house tending Maggie for some five or six years, simply wish to be company for each other."

Martha held up a finger. "Ah," she said, with an almost startled look to her expression. "There is something I now recall Maggie telling me about her own mother. Maggie was born to her father's second wife, one who had been paid companion to his first wife before she died—over many years, I seem to recall. So here, Charles, is history sort of repeating itself—in the very next generation. Oh, I am surprised at that. But I'm sure that that's the truth of things—Maggie told it me in confidence. I wonder if Ed knew. Surely he would have known it."

"Well, I can't know anything on that, Mother, one way or another. Yet it changes nowt. The way of it is that Ed has remarried. We met his Susannah at Will's funeral. Remember?"

She nodded.

I wonder if Ed could have had all that in mind even before Maggie died.

But then she shrugged her shoulders.

Such may be all right for some. But I couldn't do it. It wouldn't be right for Charles. But I'm not going to ask him what he would do. If he feels it was all right for Ed, I'd rather not hear his answer.

~ * ~

Edie gave Freddie another son they named Harold.

"Four boys, Charles. Doesn't that seem strange to you, for a mother with six sisters and only one brother?"

"Yes. But not strange for a father with three brothers and one sister."

"Mmm. Strange also, that the odd brother and the odd sister are both deceased?"

"There can be no pattern, Mother. Heredity works in strange ways."

His expression had more than a hint of annoyance in it.

It's all such a perfectly useless bloody exercise! Why does she keep persisting with it? It seems the older Mother gets, the more maudlin she becomes while I stay reasonable and even cynical about things.

Yet he quickly threw water on such thoughts when she, seemingly on cue, changed the subject.

"Walter is thinking of marrying again."

"Who to? He didn't say anything to me."

"Mary someone. A young widow."

"How old?"

"Twenty-five or six, I reckon. All he said was 'About my age.'"

"Well, it's six years since his Ann died, girl. It's about time he married again. I've kept telling him."

"Why do you think he should marry again?"

"A man needs a wife and children. That's the pattern of life, isn't it?"

He smiled on saying that. *I think my Martha has one rule for herself and another for others. She changed the subject quickly enough when it got around to thinking about why Ed might have wanted to marry again. Maybe it's the age difference that introduces differing criteria?*

"Well, I think we should just leave things until he tells us more, Charles. We shouldn't pressure the boy."

He didn't comment. He knew she liked things in neat little piles.

~ * ~

Queen Victoria had her Golden Jubilee a year after the Sydney-Newcastle rail link finally opened—fifty years on the throne during which her Empire not only became the largest in the world but the strongest and wealthiest. There was great jubilation. Charles availed himself of a Sovereign and a Half-Sovereign coin struck for the occasion. Balls and parties were held in every town, village, and hamlet throughout the nation.

Charles and Martha even hung bunting along the verandas.

The little city of Tamworth caused a furore when it scooped the pool on decorations—it won the race to become the first city on the entire continent to bathe its streets in the glow of electric lights.

"Sydney is furious, Mother," said Charles as he laid down the newspaper. "How on earth could they let a little provincial town like that pull such a fast one on our biggest city?"

But he highly applauded whatever the initiative had been. He knew Tamworth well—it was the last town on the northern line before the scarp up to the New England Plateau that had caused him so many headaches in plotting the track. It was a tiny town!

Martha smiled.

"Sydney, no doubt, had so many authorities to make their separate decisions they fell over each other's feet. That's usually the way cities work. It's happening here, Charles. I doubt we'll see Newcastle switch on electric lights in our lifetime."

"Well, I haven't been keeping up with it. Freddie will likely have a measure. He mentioned just the other day we'll one day have our railways electrified—no more locomotives, no more belching smokestacks, just wires that will kill a man if he touches them. It's all too complicated for me to grasp. I can cope with turning steam into power, but doing it all with nowt but wires and switches is beyond my ken. I'm glad it's Freddie and Walter who have to face up to these sorts of modern things."

Thirty

When Edie was large with another child, she and Freddie found their Wickham cottage too small. They settled on an imposing corner allotment in Hamilton's Lawson Street.

"I can afford it now, my sweet. The gardens are bigger for the children, and the verandas offer great potential for many more children."

"And with you now home all the time, my dearest, you've time to spend keeping the gardens in trim."

They laughed at that. Then yet again discussed how strange it seemed that none of her several births had been difficult...

"The lumbering stage has ever been my only real discomfort. And every woman has to cope with that. I just hope, darling, we continue as lucky."

And this one seemed hale. They named her Edith after her mother. And along with the bigger house, affordable with Fred's increased salary, they hired a nanny-cum-cook.

"Her arrival is timely, Freddie."

"Timely how?"

"My new interest could be time consuming."

Her singing career had quite withered since she'd started to have children. She still performed at occasional weddings and funerals, yet it had ever been clear she sought new interests.

Oh, oh! What now?

She kissed him. "You have surely read how women in the wider world, not only in Britain and America but in New Zealand and other Australian colonies, are not merely advocating the woman's right to vote—they are actually demonstrating for it?"

"Oh, the Pankhurst woman and all that? Yes, indeed. I've hesitated to mention it."

She laughed. "Well you will not be surprised, my darling, that your dear wife has found the 'coven' of suffragette 'witches' here in Newcastle. I am joining them."

He half smiled. "Without consulting me?"

She laughed aloud again. "You read me well, darling. As always. Yes—without consulting my bigoted 'man of the house,' my 'lord and master.' I intend mounting the same stages in this city as those from which I've sung, to campaign for a woman's right to have a say in what goes on in our community. I simply demand as much right as any man to decide who should represent me in parliament. And to campaign against laws demeaning womanhood."

"Is this body really a coven? And is there a name for this society of outspoken women?"

"I'm sure many men out there will insist it is a 'coven.' It is, in fact, a gentle society of learned women prepared to be anything but gentle if we don't get our way. We are determined because we are right. And the lady I have been consulting is the Newcastle president of the Australian Women's Suffrage Society."

"But do you have any bait for your hook? It is the fisherman without bait who will never catch anything. Who do you intend attacking?"

"I don't yet know about the other women, but I agree with this lady, by name Estelle, who is prepared to 'go it alone' if she cannot get others to support her. We will mount the very steps of parliament to harangue the politicians. We will insist they give our cause a hearing in the chamber."

"Parliament is in Sydney. And only elected members may take the floor. How do you overcome those obstacles?"

"We will travel to Sydney. There is a railway now, darling. Hadn't you heard?" She almost leered. "This is why I see nanny's arrival so timely. We seek not to take the floor of parliament ourselves—until elected, that is—but to influence any member who might support our campaign. Surely there are men who do not believe God gave rights to only Adam. Given one supporter, more can be recruited. And local members have local offices. We can campaign here, too."

"They may chain you to the railings of their staircases."

"Oh, please don't be crass, darling. It doesn't become you. You know what I mean."

He leaned over to kiss her.

"Yes, my dear, I willingly support what you are attempting. I am not saying 'Yes, you should do this,' I am saying you have every right to go campaigning. In fact, without having given it deep thought, I think you probably are right. It is a worthy cause. There is no man out there who does not value the input women make to his world."

She now leaned over to kiss him.

"Thank you, my darling. In fact, my first meeting is tomorrow night. I have asked nanny to serve dinner early so I can leave by seven-thirty."

Not wanting to see his reaction, she turned. In turning, she missed his reaction.

He turned because he didn't want her to see the shock on his face.

~ * ~

'Young' John Richardson, although not now so young when aged twenty-four, married and flew the family coop.

"Alone at last, Mother."

She put down her *Oliver Twist,* her third Charles Dickens novel, and took off her *pince-nez* to rub the bridge of her nose.

"You make it sound like something you've been hoping for, for years. I'm just so thankful we still have little Walter. He still needs care."

"I'm looking forward to the day he starts work so we can take board from him."

"Oh, Charles! Do you realise how exasperating you can be? If anyone else were to hear you say that, they would spread it all over Newcastle."

"Yes. And ageing fathers everywhere would sing my praises. I was sent out working when younger than him, girl. But you're right, I'm not suggesting we should be sending him out, but I'm also right in saying he's not a baby who needs constant care. He's lost his parents, yes—and despite now thirteen, he still needs family. He's my grandson too, remember, but you too should be putting your feet up at your age—not still nursing him."

She shook her head before adjusting her glasses back on her nose. *When he's in these sorts of moods, I can never get anywhere with him.*

She picked up her book and stared at the page—but her mind couldn't concentrate.

Young Walter's growing the image of his mother. Give him long hair curled in tresses and longer eyebrows, and he'd pass for Annie. Not much Jones in him.

She still felt much more the boy's mother than grandmother.

...Which isn't a foolish notion. I've always been conscious of trying to influence him, not as me, but as I see Annie would have done. I still have that role to play.

She had long ago failed to regret having an only daughter. She'd even come to grips with the disappointment of Annie dying so young. She was more conscious than she believed Charles gave her credit for of having the lad consider her as anything other than a grandma.

He even calls me 'Gran,' she explained to her alter-ego.

~ * ~

On their next daughter, Edie and Fred bestowed several given names honouring those whose blood nurtured her.

"Annie Estelle Bristow Rawes she is, Ma," Freddie told her.

"Good heavens. The 'Annie' I can understand," replied Martha, "and it is indeed a nice gesture, dear. But the 'Estelle?' And I recall your mama, Edie, telling me she was born a Rawes?"

"Yes, Ma. And her mama was a Bristow. Mama was given the names Martha Bristow Rawes. And her brother and sister were both given the Bristow-Rawes names. It was a family tradition."

Martha recalled Maggie having told her that her mother's family was 'high'... *Something to do with that second marriage of her father, I think. Or was it his first marriage?*

But it was several days later that Martha took Charles into her confidence.

"It has worried me ever since that tot was born, Charles. I understand about the bestowing the family names, I even think that is nice. And I am the first to commend Freddie in wanting to call the child after his only sister. Yet at the same time it saddens me. Every time I hear it I am going to feel unhappy about how young our own Annie was when she died. And how distressing her married life became. Could it, too, become a coincidence for this little tot? It is really worrying me, Charles."

He took a deep breath, needing to think on it before answering. It worried him, now, that Martha felt that way.

The fact she has spent days pondering on it before raising it means she doesn't see it the same way either the kids or me see it. But it's going to continue stressing her.

"You didn't voice any such feeling when they named William Arthur after our son."

"Will wasn't our only son."

He sighed deeply. "Do you know why the 'Estelle' in the name?"

"Yes. Edie told us Estelle is the name of the lady in the suffragette movement she so admires."

Martha didn't return to the Annie name during the rest of their conversation. But Charles knew it lingered in her fears.

I shall mention it to Freddie—as well as to assure him I don't agree with his ma.

And the next he realised was that suddenly, the tot, whilst still baptised Annie, was being called Estelle.

Neither he nor Martha ever mentioned, even to each other, that they'd noticed.

Thirty-one

"Your ma is infected," Charles told a surprised Freddie.

"What?"

The startled Freddie imagined her diagnosed with some fatal disease…

"Infected with the same bug as your Edie. Did you see the editorial in yesterday's *Herald*? On this woman's suffrage thing?"

"I couldn't help but see it. Edie brought it to the breakfast table—waved it under my nose."

"Well, your ma has not only snipped out the article but thumbtacked it up on our kitchen wall by her recipes. She's going to talk with Edie about how she might be able to help the movement."

Charles rolled his eyes across the entire skyline while waiting for Freddie to come to grips with what had put a smirk on his face.

"And your attitude, Pa?"

"Same as yours. Suffer in silence."

"I'm not against the ideal, Pa, which is fortunate, yet I don't want be drawn into voicing comment on it. Edie seems quite one-eyed in her attitude—it is entirely a black-or-white situation."

"The mere fact our Edie and her friends have influenced even the editor to publish this means they are not going to lie down quietly.

And there can be no half-way to it. Surely it is a case of give them the vote or don't give it. Can any man win against determined women when it comes down to seeking compromise?"

Freddie laughed. "So what does Ma feel she can do?"

"Help strike a blow for women," is what she says. She's mentioned no specific, yet would never become simply a gullible follower of anything. She's another Edie in that respect."

"They'll keep fuelling each other's fire?"

"Indeed. So far your ma has declared nowt but that she will talk with Edie—so I'm just going to wait and see. But the article up on the wall is a statement, and you know how she never backs-bloody-down on anything."

A week later the *Newcastle Herald* broke with an astounding headline.

New Zealand women given the vote!

Bloody hell, thought Charles.

There'll be no stopping them now, thought Freddie.

The *Herald* followed its headline by detailing that now the first country in the world had made its decision, others were sure to follow.

Surely, now, campaigning around the rest of the world would start steamrolling.

"Now I'm doubly determined," declared an almost defiant Martha.

Edie drove her gig to Tighe's Hill.

"Every suffragette member in Newcastle is receiving a telegram to come along to The Victoria on Friday night, Mother Martha. We expect every seat will be filled. I am going early. Will you come?"

"Indeed I will."

Edie kissed her. "I will pick you up at six-thirty."

Martha's campaign had begun.

"With her on board, lads," Charles told Freddie and John over ales at The Wickham Arms that night, "we can cut years off the time it will take New South Wales to follow New Zealand."

Freddie's brother Walter wrote from Maitland. *My Mary is haranguing women in the Maitland marketplace, and even on the platform as people wait for their train.*

"Poor young bugger," Charles told his other sons. And even though Walter's station master there, what can the poor bloody boy do than let her get away with it?"

They were at the Wickham Arms again, for all their wives were out campaigning.

"And three or four days every week they're doorknocking with pamphlets..."

"Or speaking at rallies..."

And at work Charles told his colleagues, "It's become like a bloody war at home—not an argumentative war, simply soap-box orations. Martha practises on me."

Many a man shared the same fate.

They could but share the solace that none was alone in having his domestic routine in upheaval. All quickly realised what had begun as but murmurings throughout every Australian colony had became a roar. Throughout Britain, Europe, and the Americas, women fought traditional, male-orientated influence on governments. Each insisted their country follow New Zealand's lead.

Britain stood firm, yet her empire's colonies took reins into their own hands.

Second in the world to grant the vote was the Colony of South Australia.

Edie took time out when little Edie became desperately ill. It was another case of infantile cholera. And at two years old, little Edie succumbed.

They buried her at the new cemetery of Sandgate.

Yet the mother Edie, with Fred's encouragement, used campaigning to help hide the grief. But only until autumn, when she bore the frustration of again taking time out to bring another child into the world—Lillian Bristow.

Edie and Martha, some weeks later, sat with Freddie and Charles.

Edie was champing at the bit to be back on the campaign trail. Martha was as eager, yet her age was starting to warn her to treat life with more care. Freddie's career moves now had him stationed permanently at home although also out several nights a week at classes.

Thank God for nannies, or we poor bloody husbands would be baby-sitting bairns, Charles bemoaned. At Lawson Street, Edie promised Freddie she would whittle down her time away from home.

"Estelle and I have become leaders in personally interviewing political leaders and disseminating the word at meetings. But we have been doing some reorganising as other capable women take on responsibilities. I have opted out of journeying to Sydney and will instead take on some of Estelle's planning work. I can do that at home."

All were conscious of how even the two men of the foursome, despite being early cynics and sceptics, felt it behove on them to progress the will of their nation's people.

Charles and Freddie both congratulated their wives.

"You've both showed common-sense in all this, girl," Charles told Martha. "It's high time you started acting your age, to spend more time off your feet."

At sixty-eight, she had to agree.

They spent the next night together by the fire, she returning to her *Oliver Twist*, he to his newspaper.

But bloody hell! It's all simply full of bloody suffragette nonsense, all over the bloody world!

Thirty-two

Some months later

Martha had been given little warning she was to lose him.

"It just all seemed so sudden. One minute he was here, the next, gone."

Her Charles complained of chest pains, waving off her suggestion that he stay abed.

Haven't I been hale and hearty all my life? I'm not going to start being told to stay abed when it's nowt but congestion.

It was more.

Congestion of the lungs, failure of the heart. Death sudden... was what the attending doctor noted.

Martha was in shock

It needed to be a quick funeral, for it was a hot start to summer.

"Oh, why can't he be buried at Waratah with Will and Annie?"

"It's full, Ma. Sandgate is the new cemetery. We'll buy a large plot so there's room for others. Maggie's pa has built a huge monument in Sydney where many Bourns are buried."

"Your father, Freddie, didn't care for that. He told me at the time he felt big monuments for the dead were things 'misplaced.' 'Fancy buildings are for the living to enjoy,' is what he said, so I know he wouldn't be happy with that. That's why he didn't do such for Will or Annie. 'My Pa,' he always said about big monuments, 'didn't get anything fancy when he died—best he got was a wooden cross with a simple message.'"

"What do you want to do then, Ma? A 'modest' headstone?"

"A wooden cross with a simple message," she instructed Freddie.

"And I don't want to be far behind him, boy," she added, "so when I'm laid with him, you can add whatever you like."

"Don't talk like that, Ma. I know that right now you feel you mightn't want long alone. But we all still need you around. It's not just young Walter still needs your sensible counselling."

So there was no great fanfare for the funeral.

And they didn't add 'Allison' to his name.

Ed responded to Edie's telegram with an urgent reply— the prompt funeral didn't give him time to get there. But he wired a huge floral tribute, thanking Charles for his 'stalwart friendship.'

Martha took his death philosophically. She knew that was the way he invariably felt about deaths.

"I was lucky to have him so long. And we both were lucky to enjoy good health through the years," she told the family.

"He was a good father too, Ma," Freddie replied. "It will be a good future for the world if there are more like him."

His ma smiled. "Never as much like him for you and me though, boy."

But what I will never tell my kids is how lucky I feel at being the one left. I can bear loneliness better than him. All our lives he has been the 'doer,' always about being busy while I was the one left alone. From the day we married, he was off in the field—from Goole, Glasgow, even once settled in Parramatta if you could call that 'settled.' He was ever 'in the field' or 'Up the Grose.' I was alone more years than I had him with me until all the children were born and we came to Newcastle. Yes, I can cope with loneliness. I think he was likely never lonely except for those 'lost' days Up the Grose.

He always said, after that, that he nearly went crazy with worry because he had no one to share his problems with.

"So I'm content, Charles," she said to the mantle clock, "that I've not left you lonely. I can make do until, like your furloughs in those days, we can be together again."

~ * ~

Freddie, Edie, and family quit their Hamilton house and moved in with Mother Martha.

They ensured she could enjoy a satisfying mix of hustings on the suffragette trail on the one hand and family on the other.

Edie brought two more children into the family's world during the next three years, Eric Disney Bourn and Muriel Rawes.

Martha developed an illness during these years, and the doctors suspected cancer.

She continued to lose both weight and energy, but there was little the medical profession could do other than prescribe laudanum for the pain.

As spring began blooming in gardens and parks, Freddie and Edie knew it was unlikely their dear mama would see Christmas.

On her seventy-second birthday, she told them how much she was looking forward to joining her Charles in the next world.

And the very next day, she did.

Epilogue

It was too difficult for me to write such a tale with both heroines named Martha. I apologise to Bourn and Rawes descendants that she was here called Maggie.

Two 1899 events were of particular importance to Edie. The colony of Western Australia gave its women the vote. On 7th August at the Tighe's Hill house, she gave birth to the last of her eleven children—a bawling Victor Frederick. Was the 'Victor' a celebration of the other?

As the midnight hour struck the dawn of a new century, 1st January 1901, the world welcomed a new nation. Great Britain's colonies on the 'great south land' formed a federation named 'Australia.'

The *Newcastle Directory* of 1901 lists our Charles Frederick as *NSW Railway Inspector* yet no record of his employment survives in government archives. Only one record of the Richardson family does, the lifetime employment record of the Charles Frederick Richardson born to William and Hope. It is a delightful document, from his joining on a six-month probation as 'fitter' at the princely sum of 9/6 (nine shillings and sixpence) per day in 1899, through promotions 'foreman' to 'Schedule Officer' until his retirement. The department apologised that in the move during the early 1900s of the Railways head office from the Everleigh works to the central Sydney office in York Street, many personnel records were 'lost.'

Edie died in 1902 (age forty-nine) while visiting Sydney for sister Hope's remarriage.

Ed Bourne died at his Marrickville home in 1905 (age eighty-two). He and Susannah lie in Sydney's Waverly Cemetery—their imposing monument commanding a magnificent Pacific Ocean view.

Freddie survived Edie by only seven years. He died in Newcastle Hospital and is buried alongside his parents at Sandgate. Of his surviving children, only Ted remained in Newcastle. The remaining seven moved to Sydney, where there were better employment opportunities for all. Annie Estelle subbed as mother to the littlies while older siblings took jobs. When the littlies were self-sufficient, Estelle took off for India, where she worked until retirement as a missionary. Many descendants, including Freddie and Edie's sons Victor Frederick 1940 (forty-one) and William Arthur 1951 (seventy) are buried in the Bourn Mausoleum.

Two of the carriages brought by Edward Bourn to NSW have been restored and are displayed at Powerhouse Museum in Sydney's Ultimo.

Even today, hikers and campers Up the Grose remain vulnerable to getting lost. Ground and helicopter searches are common. Some searches still prove fruitless.

The Lithgow Zig Zag is no longer part of the western line. It was replaced in 1910 by a ten-tunnel diversion. Steam-train enthusiasts, however, can still traverse it on a Blue Mountains sightseeing excursion.

Kev Richardson

Meet *Kev Richardson*

Following a career in business management at international level, Kev attained a degree in journalism, to then sweat as far up the River Nile as one can get, canoe down the Amazon, flash countless photographs from atop the Eiffel Tower, the heights above Yosemite, the Victoria Falls, *et al*, scream *"Ole"* at a Chihuahua bullfight, ride elephant trails in Thai jungles, wallow in the incredible history of Rapa Nui's Maoi—and as convention almost demands, was mugged in Bogotá. His articles on travel to exotic lands have featured in travel and airline magazines around the world.

Meanwhile, being a sixth-generation descendant from Australia's First Fleet with an obsessive interest in his country's founding, he was disappointed at generations of suppression in the hidden truths of that history. Years of fact-finding, with the help of other dedicated researchers, revealed all, and Kev vowed to set the history books aright by bringing the truths of convictism to light. He is well qualified to do so, for as a student of First Fleet history, he has presented his subject on many occasions in press, radio, and television interviews. He is a past president of *The First Fleet Fellowship* and a past secretary of *The Descendants of Convicts Inc.* During Australia's 1988 Bicentenary, he officiated in Founding celebrations in Sydney, Melbourne, Hobart, and Norfolk Island. For his work during that Bicentenary, he was created honorary life member of *The Regiment of Redcoat Descendants*.

Kev now devotes his life to writing on not only his country's convict history and general fiction with an Australian flavour, but biographies of significant people. He recognises the growing trend towards digital reading, so follows the world's top authors in publishing his works both as traditional paperbacks and the economical eBook.

His *Gurrewa* (two books in the series), *Brogan* (four books in the series) and his *Letitia Munro* trilogy, all released by *Wings-Press (wingsepress.com)*, include awards-winners and five-star reviews. Synopses of all works can be read on www.kev.richardson.com. Three biographies are contracted for release during 2010.

These days Kev travels less, having retired from his home on Queensland's Gold Coast and left his grown family and friends to write from experiences and adventures during his exciting travels, happily ensconced in the foothills of the Golden Triangle in amazing Thailand's exotic north.

Other Works from the Pen of

Kev Richardson

Gurrewa - Finalist in the 2002 Independent eBook Awards. A true story of the shame of a nation's founding. It empties the vacuum cleaner after the Australian authorities of the day had swept the dust of truths under the carpet. Adam lives the shame of those days.

ADAM—Son of Gurrewa - A tale of discovery in New South Wales. The children of convicts discover how Australia is indeed the lucky country. Adam helps lead it to its burgeoning wealth in both real and personal riches. Convict traits emerge to create unique personal attitudes in their new land.

Brogan - A tale of life on Australia's desert edge. In the early 1900s, Australia was a nation in transition. Brogan, born in the drifting sands of the far outback, exemplifies the blood-and-guts characteristics by which Aussies are recognised even today.

Brogan's Bust: Brogan, enmeshed in intrigue, flies a courier service in the Amazonian jungles, where graft and corruption make mockery of the law. Backstabbing amongst cartel middlemen, goaded by greed, turn a hiccup into a stumble that generates into a fall to begin a slide that snowballs into an avalanche.

Brogan's Bella - Isabella and Brogan are victims in a deadly hijack. Their carefree, leisurely trip through Pacific Islands becomes a nightmare of death and terror. Their holiday turns into a year of incarceration and intimidation, embroiled in the cutthroat intrigue of jungle politics and guerrilla warfare, or facing the cutting of their own throats for even knowing the truths behind the hijack.

Brogan Abroad - A modern Brogan finds himself embroiled in three simultaneous adventures, planning none yet finding each destines him to having his throat slit in some dark alley. "Yet what can a man do," he laments, "when to accomplish one I must fail at another?" He juggles hiding in Thailand from a Sydney drug cartel with smuggling a high-profile prostitute into Australia as well as being hijacked in third-world Sudan as it counts down the hours to bloody revolution.

Letitia Munro - A true tale of Australia's first white settlement, of those who in witless ignorance transform the world's biggest prison into a land of free enterprise and pride. Ignominy of servitude bred in them irrefragable support for underdogs, determination of purpose towards mateship, and their flippant attitude to authority and class distinction.

To Plough Van Diemen's Land - Children of convicts spawn a new ethos. Titia's descendants, illiterate and utterly unskilled, must learn everything by surviving hard knocks and bad luck. Some fail, unaware of the social taboos being woven into the nation's spawning culture.

The Terrible Truths - Third in the *Letitia Munro* trilogy finds the children and grandchildren swept up in the traumas as society values change, of having to hide the truths of their heritage—and to begin coping with the growth of industry beginning to shake world economies. Australia begins emerging as a veritable beehive of mines as minerals of every description begin showering riches on the land.

A Welcome War - World War II was the most welcome and alluring war of all time. A ten-year-old lad begins his next six years influenced more by military strategy, political power, and bathos than by parents or mentors. As a means of discovering how people react to adverse situations, and as fundamental lessons of history and geography are taught him in the most alluring ways—to put in his own words, "It beats schoolwork, hands down!"

Gerard Rawes (November 2010) - Gerard finds his life transformed from rags to riches, and discovers how circumstances can pluck a man from one situation, to drop him in another—as a tsunami can pluck a body from a beach and seemingly cast it up on the shore of a distant world. In England's mid-eighteenth century, the emerging industrial revolution catapults Gerard out of his world of serfdom into London's elite. A true-life biography.

Letter to Our Readers

Enjoy this book?

You can make a difference

As an independent publisher, Wings ePress, Inc. does not have the financial clout of the large New York Publishers. We can't afford large magazine spreads or subway posters to tell people about our quality books.

But, we do have something much more effective and powerful than ads. We have a large base of loyal readers.

Honest Reviews help bring the attention of new readers to our books.

If you enjoyed this book, we would appreciate it if you would spend a few minutes posting a review on the site where you purchased this book or on the Wings ePress, Inc. webpages at: https://wingsepress.com/

Visit Our Website

For The Full Inventory
Of Quality Books:

Wings ePress.Inc
https://wingsepress.com/

Quality trade paperbacks and downloads
in multiple formats,
in genres ranging from light romantic comedy
to general fiction and horror.
Wings has something for every reader's taste.
Visit the website, then bookmark it.
We add new titles each month!

Wings ePress Inc.
3000 N. Rock Road
Newton, KS 67114